# 1

# I am God.

There is no greater joy in all the world than killing someone. Watching the light fade out of their eyes is a feeling that has no equal. It's almost erotic in the waves of pleasure it delivers.

I'll never forget the first time. I was barely more than a kid. I had been practicing on animals for years, but it wasn't enough anymore. I was craving... more. One day the opportunity presented itself. It basically fell into my lap, honestly.

There was a homeless man who had been living in the woods behind our family property. I found him bent over the creek one morning and snuck up behind him. I bashed his head in with a giant rock and the wet crunch of bone and brain matter was exhilarating in ways I never imagined it could be.

He made a grunt as he slumped over face-first into the water. At first, I let him lay there and watched as his body twitched and wiggled, trying to breathe through an inch of flowing water that was slowly turning red as the blood seeped from his head. When I finally turned his body over, I stared straight into his eyes while I smashed that rock into his head over and over. I can still picture the exact moment his soul left him.

I got scared when it was all done and over. The high wore off and I started to worry about being caught. The day the cops got called out to bring in the body I think I almost shit myself, but then nothing happened. No news story. No gossip in town. That's when I knew I could get away with it and that high was almost as good as killing him.

I felt like God.

That opened up whole new worlds for me. I knew that I could do whatever I wanted and I did just that, though increasingly more carefully and well planned out for the most part. I began to build a new life and I blossomed in it. I had officially found my calling. I've been living it ever since and have never once come close to being caught.

Maybe I am God.

AMANDA EAST

# Home is Where the Bodies Are

# I

## GONE

*"No one ever told me that grief felt so like fear."*
*–C.S. Lewis*

# 2

# Savannah

Small towns have an odd kind of charm during the warmer months of the year. They are beautiful, cozy, and welcoming with their bright green lawns and smiling faces walking the sidewalks. They appear just like you would expect Mayberry to look and feel, American as apple pie, but then the winter comes. The cold strips away the green of the trees and the friendly mystique of the once busy streets. Everything becomes barren and unforgiving with no pleasantries to cover your dirty laundry on the line.

That is how I remember my hometown. I do not memorialize the sun-soaked summers. I remember the cold, frigid bite of its true nature instead. I left for a reason. I have even managed to go at least the last few days without thinking of it at all until I looked down at my phone screen just now to see that 4-1-7 area code indicating a call from the town I've been running from for ten years. Just like that, it all came flooding back in a rush of anxiety.

Do I answer? Let it go to voicemail so I can stare at it in my inbox and let it torture me endlessly until I listen? Well, shit.

"Hello?"

"This is James River Rehabilitation and Long Term Care. May I please speak with Savannah Raymore?"

"This is she."

"Ms. Raymore, I am calling in regards to Jack Raymore who is a patient in our facility. Your brother has requested that we call to inform you that end of life care has been initiated. He is asking for you."

Thoughts of my father immediately send me reeling into that black hole of the past. At least it's good news. He's finally going to be dead.

"My father wants me there or my brother?"

"Your brother has asked for you, ma'am."

Well, he can go fuck himself, I think to myself. As I prepare to tell the young girl on the other end of the phone just that, I hear rustling as she places her hand over the receiver to whisper to someone in her world. She is trying to muffle her conversation but I still hear her loud and clear.

"Have a great day, Officer Perez!"

My breath catches in my chest and I immediately dislike this complete stranger for the smile in her voice as she says his name. Before I even know what I'm doing, "I'll be there tomorrow," has slipped out of my mouth and I hang up the phone. What just happened?

I stand in stunned silence and stare at the phone in my hand. I just agreed to go see my father. I haven't spoken to him since the day I left town and had no intention to ever again, yet I hear the last name Perez and I'm ready to head straight there. I don't even know if it's him. It could be anyone that shares his last name. It's not that uncommon. I want to roll it off of me and pretend like I can just decide not to go, but I can't. I know

I'll go. Call me a masochist, but I have to go and find out what became of the life I ran away from. I didn't even know I was craving that until this very second. The thought fills me with more exhilaration than I have felt in years. I know it will hurt, but at least I will feel something.

My current state of numb has become too much. The buzz I feel now as I begin randomly throwing whatever I can grab from my closet into the first bag I lay my hands on makes me feel frantic in glorious ways. The anxiety of it charges me up for the first time in forever. It feels like I'm moving at warp speed, but I don't realize how accurate that is until I hear my name from the doorway.

"Savannah," Colby calls from the entrance to our bedroom, "Everything okay?"

I freeze like a child who just got caught pilfering money from her parents' wallet. Simply looking at him standing there makes me feel completely vile. He is beautiful and kind and caring, yet here I stand preparing to chase my past in the opposite direction. I still my manic pace and slump my shoulders as he comes to me in an attempt to comfort the crazy out of me. It's basically useless because I already know I'm going anyway. The diamond ring he put on my finger feels like hot lead against my skin at the thought.

"I have to go back home for a while," I mumble as I bury my head in his chest. I feel his whole body tense as this sinks in.

He has an edge to his voice as he asks, "Why would you want to do that?"

"Dad is dying. Shane asked for me and I feel like going is the right thing to do." Surely he won't see through my half-truth. That is part of the reason.

He pulls back and looks deeply into my face as if trying to

decipher my real thoughts and feelings beneath the mask I wear every day. After a long pause, "I think it's great that you want to move past what your dad did, but I'm worried going back home might be too much for you..."

Something in that statement makes me bristle and wiggle out of his arm's length grasp, "I'm a big girl. I'll be fine."

Colby is taken aback by my reaction, "That's not how I meant it and you know it," he says as he pulls me back toward him. Looking down into my face, he places a gentle hand on my stomach, "I just know you're already stressed about how long it's taking us to put a baby in there. I don't want you to put anything else on your plate right now." His smile is so sweet, but it makes my stomach sour.

About that... I don't know how in the world to tell him that I really have no desire to accomplish that goal right now. Being a mom isn't something I have ever really wanted, but I can't bring myself to break his heart with that. He wants it so much that... I don't know how to say no. I avoid the question instead, "This is just something I need to do, okay?"

He chews his lip and sits on the edge of our bed as I go back to packing, "Then I'll go with you."

Suddenly it is perfectly clear to me that I don't want him to come with me and I'll say whatever it takes to make that happen. I roll my eyes, "You don't want to go back there any more than I do and you know that right now is the absolute worst time for you to miss work. All you've talked about for weeks is making partner. You are working so many insane hours that I'll be back before you know I'm gone."

He looks grumpy at my refusal, "I don't feel right letting you go back alone."

I release a deep sigh and sit by his side. Winding my fingers through his I get to the bottom line that I didn't even realize was there, "I haven't spoken to my brother in 5 years. I miss him. I think it's time for me to go back and fix that. I need to do that alone."

There is more truth in that statement than I even realized. Wow. I really do miss my brother. We let our feelings about what Dad did get between us and I have so much regret about that. I am filled with melancholy letting myself think about it. Tears fill my eyes and I think Colby has relented because he starts helping me pack. We finish filling my bags with much more sensible items than I was packing alone and he loads them in my car. While he is downstairs, I call the library I work in to let them know I will be out of town for a bit. They are very understanding when I tell them the dire state of my father's health. I'll leave it at that. They don't need the gory details. When Colby gets back upstairs he still looks worried.

"I'll be fine, I promise," I tell him with pleading eyes.

He kisses my hand and toys with the ring on my finger, "Are you still going to be wearing this when you get back?"

His question catches me off guard and makes heat rise into my cheeks. I thought I was the only one of us that had wondered what might happen if I encountered my old love, the love I had run from, but my new love had been contemplating that as well. The realization crushes me, but not enough to stop me from going. I am an awful human being.

"Colby, I will come back to you. I promise."

As he hugs me so tight and kisses my hair, I tell myself that I will keep that promise. Even if it kills me.

# 3

## She will be mine.

Savannah is the grand prize. I've watched her for as long as I can remember. It's like she is the complete antithesis to what I am. I am death. She is life.

I didn't fall in love with her all at once. It was over years of memories together. The way she throws her head back when she laughs. The kind things she does just because. Her brown hair shining in the sun. How she gets completely lost in the books she's always reading. The supple fullness in all the curves of her body. The way she glows when she's talking to a child. Everything about her is magic.

In the beginning, I only watched her when we were already in the same place at the same time. She would walk in and time would slow down for me. I had to see what she would do and say. She slowly crept into my mind and took over every thought. I started to plan where I was going based on where I thought she would be. It became a game for me. When I guessed right and saw her somewhere, I would reward myself by following her home. It didn't take long, though, before that wasn't enough either. I had to have more of her.

I needed to be in her world. I made friends with her friends, played the part she needed me to be to fit into her life. I got in and suddenly had access to her all the time. If I hadn't known I was in love with her before, I did then. I knew life would never be complete without her in it.

He is the only thing in my way. Somehow, she loves us both and I can't have that. I've thought about killing him a million different ways, but that wouldn't solve my problem. That would only give him more power. He would be forever memorialized in her heart. I don't want her to mourn him. I want her to hate him. I won't share her heart with him so I'll just have to ruin him instead.

She was going to be mine.

She still will be mine.

I will make her mine.

# 4

# Savannah

During the fall of my 16th year, my mother disappeared off the face of the planet. She literally just vanished. It was like the cruelest of all magic tricks. One day she was there and then she just wasn't anymore.

We were at a carnival that night. I was there with my boyfriend. Mom was there with Dad. My brother, Shane, had been working which is something he has regretted ever since. He has asked himself over and over, could he have made it different? Could he have prevented it from happening at all if he had been there? I torture myself with the same kind of questions. If I had been paying more attention to life outside my bubble, would I have seen it all unfolding? Could I have stopped it? Would she still be here?

That was the thing too. No one had seen anything that night. How does a grown woman vanish without anyone seeing anything?

There was so much speculation over what happened and everyone helped us search for her at first. Eventually, though, the search party shrank. Then it shrank some more until all that was left was me and Shane. There was so little to go on that everyone decided she had just run away. She had gotten tired of her alcoholic husband and walked away from her whole life for a new start.

There will never be a world in which I believe that. She wasn't that person. She was an amazing mother. She was my best friend. She was both our cheerleader and our total support system, our hand to hold in the dark. There was nothing she loved more than being our mom. She never would have left us.

Shane and I were on the same page with that. He knew she didn't leave us, but he was also certain our father had nothing to do with her disappearance. I can't say I ever felt the same.

Dad was with her that night. He was holding her hand the last time I saw her being swallowed up by the crowd. He was home alone and drunk out of his mind when we got home and realized she was gone. It was him. I have zero doubt.

My constant need to express that when I was an impulsive teenager was the first crack in mine and Shane's relationship. When I finally moved away at 20, we tried to keep up with each other for so long but the still angry burn of our loss tore the rest of our relationship to the ground. Really, I did that pretty well on my own. I was in so much pain that I didn't know how to not lash out when he tried to reason with me. I'm older now and I think I can manage a renewed relationship with him as long as he's willing to give me another chance.

Dialing his number right now feels like second nature. There was a time when my brother was the most important person in my life. With each ring, I can feel the tension building in my shoulders out of fear that he might just want nothing to do with me anymore. Maybe he only asked the nursing home to call me out of sheer obligation.

Then, through the phone, comes a familiar male voice, "Hello?"

Hearing him speak for the first time in half a decade, I forget how to talk for a minute. Finally, I say, "Hi Shane."

"Holy shit. Is that really you Savvy?"

"It's me." I smile and feel little prickly tears sting my eyes as I hear the relief in his voice.

"I take it they called you about dad?"

"They did."

"You calling to tell me to fuck off then?"

We both laugh and I respond, "Actually, I was wondering if I could stay with you when I get there."

"Wait. Seriously? You're really coming?"

"Only if you're okay with it."

"Of course I'm okay with it. You can even have your old room back. Move in if you want," he says with a laugh.

"You're still in mom and dad's house?"

"Yeah. Just doesn't feel right to sell it." We're both silent for a moment before he continues, "Just waiting for you to come hang out again I guess. It's been too long, Savvy."

"I know. I... I'm on my way now. Surprise. "

I can hear his smile, "Awesome. I'll keep an eye out for you."

As we hang up the phone, I grip the steering wheel a little tighter. Am I ready for this? Every mile makes it feel a little more real.

As I get closer and closer the land seems to morph into the land I grew up on. No more busy city streets. No more flat, spanning farmland. I grew up surrounded by giant hills, forever green with cedars and pine, rocky cliff sides stretching tall along the roads where passages were blasted through the once mountains.

The Ozarks.

I have forgotten how much I love the land here. Seeing it for the first time in so long is a painful reminder of all the good I have left behind as well. Suddenly, I remember it wasn't all bad here, there was just so much bad that I abandoned it all, even the parts I loved.

The year my mom left was the beginning of the end for me and my town. Without her in it, it was just never the same. She was the heart of our family. She was so beautiful. Everyone says I look just like her, but I will never shine and sparkle as she did. She was pure and joyful in everything she ever did. Losing her killed that part of me.

I can't think of her and concentrate on driving. I wipe a tear from my cheek and shake off that particular part of my past. It's just too much. Instead, I shift to my father. I don't even know if I will be able to look at him. He's why she is gone. He was a drunk most of my life and he was never good to her.

Shane remembered more of the dad he was before the accident that stole his essence from us. He fought me every step of the way when I would rant about Dad's guilt, but my boyfriend, Cash, hadn't cared if I was right or wrong. He had been my pillar of strength in the storm. I knew during those first whirlwind months of missing my mother that I would never want to marry anyone but my Cash. Maybe that's why I never have. I have been engaged for three years and just can't bring myself to set a date. I've never been able to move past that mindset. Watching Cash move on without me should have pushed me forward in itself, but I think it stunted my ability to have a healthy relationship instead.

I release a deep sigh, trying to wrap my head around what the hell I am doing, as I pass the city limit sign I haven't seen since that day I left. I really did drive away and never look back. I wonder now, as I go down streets I still know like the back of my hand, how different my life might look if I had allowed myself second thoughts. Even just once. Would I still be stuck here? Would that be so bad?

I pass all the landmarks of my early life and find myself smiling to spite myself. The road closes in on itself a little tighter. The shoulder of the road morphs into grassy ditches. I soak in the hollow sound of driving across the old iron bridge over Bull Shoals Lake and feel a thrill to see the water churning restlessly all around me. It all fills my soul to the brim.

The nostalgia increases even more as I turn into the rural wooded neighborhood that holds my childhood home. I rode my bike alongside my mom on these dusty gravel roads. I had my first kiss under that oak tree right there. I crashed my car into that street sign leading to the loop my parents called home. I cried myself to sleep the night mom didn't come home just beyond that little dormer window on that house right there.

Pulling in the driveway feels surreal. Seeing my brother step out onto the front steps is even crazier. An uncontrollable smile spreads across my face as I step out of my car. I was unsure of how our first reunion would feel, but as we walk directly into a warm embrace all fears of awkwardness wash away. I melt into the warm comfort of family. I have missed this so much.

"I'm really glad you're home," he says.

With sincerity dripping from my words, I tell him, "I'm really glad I came."

We've been through so much together and we let it get to us for a long time. We let it divide our family, at least what's left of it, and this reunion goes to show we're both ready to make amends. Really, I'm the only one who needs to make amends.

"I'm really sorry, Shane."

He shakes his head and gives my shoulder a shove, "We're not doing that. We're good. Always will be."

# 5

## I couldn't let her go.

I was looking for a carnie. I just wanted to find some stranger from who knows where that wouldn't be missed. That was my goal for the night. I found so much more.

She was standing behind the trailer that housed the funhouse. Flashing lights from the Ferris wheel lit her hair and her face just enough for my brain to register Savannah's name loud and clear. She was smoking a cigarette. I had never seen her do that before. I hate smokers. You would think it would completely repulse me, right?

Turns out I like a little fire in my girl.

I watched her for what felt like hours but it must have only been a few seconds. My breath seemed to be stuck in my throat. I could feel my jeans tighten as my dick hardened uncontrollably. I knew I had to have her. I couldn't wait. It had to be then, so I took her.

I had her right there. I shoved her against that trailer and took what was meant to be mine. She may have given it freely if she knew it was me, but I wanted to know what it felt like to just take it. Turns out, it felt even better than killing someone.

It took me by complete surprise when I realized it wasn't actually her. My head had wrapped itself up into the fantasy and until it was over I just didn't realize the sound of her screaming didn't quite match my Savannah.

In my shock, I turned her body to face mine and locked eyes with the wrong girl. The moment I realized what I had just done was the same moment recognition lit up her crying eyes.

I knew I couldn't let her go home now.

# 6

# Savannah

Waking up in my old bedroom and walking down the stairs I spent the first twenty years of my life climbing is completely bizarre. Shane is already in the kitchen with a full breakfast spread prepared and it isn't even 8:30 AM. So freaking weird.

"Since when are you an early riser," I ask.

"Since I have been a teacher for the last ten years."

"But, like, it's Saturday..."

He rolls his eyes at me and places a plate of pancakes, bacon, eggs, and hashbrowns in front of me. "I supervise Saturday school for any kids who need internet access for homework on the weekends."

I smile at this, "Aren't you a regular hometown hero?"

"Shut up and eat, Savvy."

"Actually, I really just want some coffee."

"You know that stuff will kill you, right?"

I crinkle my nose and glance down at the edible heart attack on the plate before me, "And this won't?" I've earned another eye-roll, but I can tell we both enjoy the back and forth banter that we haven't taken part in for so long. "It's really nice to be back here."

"I'm glad. Dad will love to hear your voice. He's missed you too, you know."

Now it's my turn to roll my eyes, but I hold the bitterness inside, "How long has he been in the facility?"

"Just the last two years. He had a stroke and wasn't really ever the same after that, couldn't really take care of himself. I moved back in and lived with him for about a year, but then it just became too much. A couple of really good friends convinced me to take him to James River. It's a nice place and they take really good care of him. Better care than I could give him."

Too bad... "So you stayed here after he went there?"

"Yeah. It was nice to be here in this house again. It still feels like Mom here."

We share a smile. It does feel like her here. Nothing has been changed since the day she left and I can still see her little touches everywhere. It's wonderful.

I laugh to myself and ask, "Do you remember when we wanted to clean the house really good so mom would take us to Branson for the weekend and we were out of dishwasher stuff so we put Dawn dish soap in instead?"

Shane laughs now too, "And we didn't notice until it was *way* too late?"

"Mom walked in from work and just stared at her kitchen full of bubbles and then walked away like she hadn't seen it at all until she came back with goggles and a snorkel on. She dove right into the bubbles like it was the most normal thing ever."

We're both laughing now, but it turns bittersweet so fast. "She was the best," he says.

"She was."

A few moments of silence descend on us until Shane clears his throat, "So how's big city life treating you?"

I pause, deciding whether to be honest or keep things upbeat, "It's great. I walk through this gorgeous park on my way to work every day. I work in the gigantic library right in the middle of downtown. It's really great."

"Good. I'm glad. I was really hoping you were happy. You've got people there too? I know the first few years you were pretty isolated. People to be there for you when you need it?"

I take a hard swallow. I knew this part was coming, "Um... yeah. I have people, or rather someone. I have a someone."

Shane seems to have noticed my engagement ring for the first time as I toy with it on my finger, "Is that...?"

"Yeah. I'm engaged and we live together and it's really great." He looks sad now and I feel awful. I never even called to tell him I was engaged. I've never told him anything about my life with Colby. He doesn't even know Colby is a part of my life at all.

"Wow. Savvy, that's awesome. I hope he's everything you are looking for."

"Well, you know him or knew him I guess, actually. He's from here. It's the wildest story... I had been there for years all by myself and we weren't talking anymore and," I know I'm rambling now, but I'm so nervous, "someone broke into my apartment one night while I was sleeping and-"

"Please don't tell me he was the burglar?"

I giggle nervously, "Oh my gosh, no. No, he saved me from the burglar. He was the new neighbor and he heard me yelling and the bad guy ran out the window when he broke down my front door to save me and-"

"Spit it out, Savvy."

I take a deep breath and swallow again, "I could hardly believe

22

it when he ran in with a baseball bat over his head. I never imagined seeing a familiar face."

"And that face was?"

"It was Colby Adams."

"Are you fucking kidding me?" Shane asks as he starts slinging dishes into the sink with annoyance.

"He's really great, Shane. Seriously. You would love him now. He's grown up so much and he is so good to me. Better than I deserve."

"He was the most annoying little twat to ever reside in the state of Missouri. He wanted to be all up in everybody's business all the time and his whole nice guy act was so fucking phony, Savvy."

"It wasn't really. He was just in a bad time at home back then. None of us knew what his house was like. We thought he had everything until his dad went to jail. We had no idea what he was going through then. He was just trying to fit in because he didn't fit in at home." Shane's eye-roll has now progressed to the super eye-roll and I can tell he doesn't believe a single word I'm saying. "You don't know him anymore. You never really did. You can't judge a stranger."

My use of one of Mom's favorite lines throws him off-kilter and softens him some, "He's good to you?"

"So good, Shane. He is an architect and he is about to become a partner at his firm and he works so hard so I can do the work I love but still live a really good life. They don't pay you a lot at the public library, Shane..." We're staring each other down across the counter to see which one of us breaks first. I knew this was going to be a hard conversation and am so thankful Colby isn't here for it.

He really was insufferable when we were kids. The only child of the richest family in town and he had everything he could ever want, or so we thought. It wasn't until his dad went to prison for tax evasion and money laundering then his mom overdosed on prescription painkillers that the facade finally crumbled. He hadn't had it so great after all and who he is now is so far from who he pretended to be then.

"What time is it?" Shane asks sulkily.

I'm thrown off by the randomness of his question, "What?"

"What time is it?"

I glance at my phone, "8:20."

He takes my untouched plate from me, "You better get going if you're still planning to go see dad today."

"I was going to eat some of that and I don't think he's going anywhere..."

"All the good parking spots get taken if you don't get there early enough," he says as he pulls my chair up from under me and ushers me toward the door. "Go on. Get out of here." I want to take offense or fear that he's mad about Colby, but he smiles and gives me a hug as he pushes me out the door. "You're still welcome back after even if you have terrible taste in men."

Oh, gee, thanks... I'll get there when I get there, and only after I have stopped to fully caffeinate and feed myself...

# 7

# What have I done?

hat have I done?

Savannah cries all the time. I can't believe I was so careless. I let my needs get the better of me. What if someone saw me? What if someone heard her? Everyone within 50 miles or more is looking for her. There are missing person flyers everywhere. I've even helped hang them up!

I've held Savannah while she cried. It broke me inside. I did that to her. Seeing her so heartbroken was too much so I pledged to her that I would kill the bastard that did this horrible thing and I think I meant it. Maybe I will. I'll just blow my brains out and never face this horrible thing I have done, never have to see that look of pain in my Savannah's eyes ever again. What the fuck have I done?

What if I didn't hide her well enough and they find her body filled with my DNA?

Fuck, fuck, FUCK!!!

The others weren't like this. No one looked for them. Everyone is looking for Beth, but I couldn't just let her go. She had seen my face. She would tell Savannah and everyone else and then I would never have what I have been working towards my whole life. I would never have Savannah. This cannot be happening. I may have thrown all my plans away for 60 seconds of pleasure. If Savannah finds out, she will never forgive me. She will hate me.

# 8

# Savannah

There's a stark difference between the warm home I left this morning and this old nursing home I'm walking through now. Where home smells of coffee and my mom's hugs, this place smells of antiseptic and decay. What a perfect setting for the black rotting soul that is my father. Whatever was up Shane's ass for me to get here earlier was flat out denied by my own sense of self-care and I'm glad I didn't come earlier. I'm definitely thankful for this heavy dose of espresso and preparation before I see the man that raised me.

Standing over him now is profoundly devastating. I once loved him so much and as much as I hate him now, he is still my father. Once upon a time, he was even a very good father, back before he became a stranger in my daddy's body. He was broad and strong then. He would snatch me off the ground and put me on his shoulders like I was no more than a few pounds. He would do push-ups with me and Shane on his back and carry our giggling mother up the stairs like they were newlyweds. But then it all fell apart.

He was out late at night walking our dog when a drunk driver hit him and left him for dead in a snow-filled ditch. We didn't know what happened until our worried mother went out into the cold to look for him. I was only 7 years old when it happened, but I will never forget my mom's anguished screams for 911 when she found her husband's cold and broken body laying in blood-stained snow.

He was never the same after that. The doctor said he had recovered but his body and mind were forever altered. Steel rods placed in his legs insured he would always walk with a limp and a cane. The head injury left him in a coma for 3 weeks and then with a huge mental deficit forever after. Even at the end of rehabilitation, his mind and body were never the same. That was probably the biggest injury to him, knowing he would never again be the man he had been. That made him bitter and angry. He started drinking heavily and the man I once knew as my daddy was gone forever.

The angry man he became is gone now too. Lying here in this bed, machines whirring and buzzing all around him, he just looks old and frail. I'm not afraid of him anymore and seeing him like this makes it hard to hate him too. He just looks pitiful, but I think if I look past the years of pain between us, and in his unguarded state, I can see a little of the man that used to love me more than life. Then, just as I think my heart may soften for him at the end of his life, his lips part and a single word escapes.

Beth.

Tears fall down my cheeks and bile rises in my throat to hear my mother's name from the mouth of the man that made her disappear. Here he sleeps peacefully awaiting a death brought to him by old age while she rots away wherever he stashed her body all those years ago. He doesn't have a right to speak her name. It just isn't fair. All my sympathy vanishes and hot, bitter hate fills me from the soles of my feet to the top of my head until I feel like I may explode. I leave the room in a disgusted panic.

Once in the hallway, I feel like I'm not suffocating under the weight of what he did, but I can't shake the violent throbbing growl that escapes me as I burst through the closed-off space and out toward the exit. I throw myself out into the cool day to find I'm only in the fenced-in employee smoking area and can't actually escape. I release a frustrated snarl. Why the hell had I ever thought seeing him again would be easy? Bracing myself on my knees, I hang my head until the blood rush makes the nauseous hate subside, even if just a little. I can feel the spiteful heat slowly receding as there is a metallic click behind me. A gentle hand touches my shoulder. He is an orderly from the facility and couldn't be older than 20, the age I was when I left this whole mess behind. In this moment, I remember exactly why.

"Are you okay, ma'am?"

A dry laugh escapes me. I will probably never be okay. I've definitely never been okay before, "I'm fine. Thank you."

"He sure has a way of doing that to people."

"I bet he does," I say with a dry laugh.

"Are you with the police too?" he asks.

I shake my head, "He's my father. Or at least he was at some point. I'm not really sure what he is now."

"Dang, girl. I'm sorry."

Suddenly, I register what he asked me, "What do you mean, am I with the police too?"

"Oh, there's a cop here almost every day. He usually spends at least an hour here with Mr. Raymore. He gets upset with him sometimes too."

A light bulb goes on over my head, "Always the same cop?"

"Oh yeah. Good-looking guy. Probably 6' 2", jet black hair, really dark eyes. Definitely Latino. I wish he would come visit me," he finishes wistfully. " He actually just left here about 20 minutes ago. Gotta love a man in uniform..."

The bulb burns so brightly over my head that it might burst into flames. I know I'm being rude as I walk away without a word, but I just found the perfect outlet for my fury and I want to personally deliver it before it loses any heat.

* * *

Seeing him again might have played a big part in the reasons I wanted to come home after so many years. Who am I kidding? I know that was most of it. I thought I would have so much hesitation and worry about seeing him the first time. Who knew all it would take is wanting to kill him? I take no time slinging my car into a parking space, slamming my door shut, and marching into the police station like I own the damn place. I have every intention of demanding to see Officer Perez at the front desk, but I don't even need to. I see him. He hasn't changed even a little bit. Shit. This may have been a mistake.

I must look like a lunatic. Seeing him steals my breath and I have frozen to my spot. He must feel my gaze because he looks up from his work and our eyes meet through the security glass between us. His mouth drops open just a little and I can't help but smile at his reaction. He stands and walks toward me without breaking eye contact and I think I might pass out. Whatever it was that drew us together all those years ago is clearly still here. I chew on my lip and fidget as he scans his ID badge to pass through the security door. How is it possible that

I feel 15 again right now?

The moment he passes through the security door the energy in the room completely changes. I feel hot and anxious for him to make it across the room to me. As he does, I stop noticing anything else happening around me except his body gliding toward me. I know that body like the back of my hand. Standing in front of me, we stare wordlessly at one another. He's so close that I think I can feel his body heat. We both seem to match our shallow breathing and he's looking at me like he thinks I might be a mirage.

"Are you really real?" he asks in a hushed whisper. His voice sends me into a tailspin of nostalgia. I want to reach out and feel him. I want him to feel me. I want to know if his touch still makes the world stop spinning for me.

Suddenly a phone rings shrilly near us and I'm back in the reality of this busy public place. I realize I need to get ahold of myself. I came here for a reason just like I left him behind once upon a time for a reason too.

"Why do you go see my dad? You know better than anyone how I feel about him," needing to numb my desire to press my lips against his, I throw in for good measure, "Haven't you hurt me enough?"

He jumps back as if he's been slapped and his eyes flash. I instantly feel bad, but I can't take it back. He shakes his head and brings his face even closer to mine, "I don't owe you a single thing." His hushed aggression gives me chills, "You disappeared out of my life without a goddamn word." Yelling now, he continues, "I haven't seen you in ten fucking years!"

I think flames may be shooting from our ears at this point as I yell back, "Don't you dare act like you don't know why I left." Everyone in the station has turned to stare at us now, but neither of us seems to care.

"Why don't you finally share that little tidbit of information with me so I can decide when I stopped knowing who you are," he yells back in my face.

"Stopped knowing who I am? You are the one-"

There's a startling loud bang on the security glass and we both turn to look. A tall, bald, and very important looking man lets us know with just a look that we need to shut up or leave. I turn back to Cash with anger boiling out of my pores, but it still hurts me inside to see how bitter he looks. Especially feeling that I had a hand in making him that way.

"Vannah..." hearing him use the nickname only he has ever used does things to me, "I have dreamed about the moment you would finally come home a million times," his face is close to mine now but his words are full of spite, "but never one time did I imagine it would be like this." He turns without another word and disappears behind the violent slam of a door that makes me jump.

As I turn to leave as well, I tell myself I can't believe he would have the audacity to act like I'm the unreasonable, crazy one. I let that thought sink its teeth into me and the hot fury bubbles up in me again, but this time it has a companion. Part of me wants to stab my ex-lover, the other part of me wants to take him to bed. The need in me is so white-hot that I have no idea which part is going to win the fight, but I can say I have never been so turned on in all my life and that makes me even more furious.

* * *

The whole car ride back to my brother's house, I have done

nothing but marinate in all the reasons I have to hate Cash Perez and all the reasons I can't bring myself to do that which pisses me off in serious ways. Pulling into the drive, I see a car I don't immediately recognize because I am genuinely that mad, but then it clicks. That is Colby's car. Colby is here.

Fuck my life.

I park and lay my head against the steering wheel. Now is not the best moment for this reunion. I don't have the energy to deal with the relationship I'm currently in when the heat and fire of the one I ran away from just came crashing back in on me like a landslide. Unfortunately, the current one hits me straight in the face too as I walk in on my brother interrogating Colby like he's under oath.

"Do you think maybe she didn't invite you for a reason?" Shane asks.

Colby is painfully defensive, "Look, we've been together long enough that I just feel the need to protect her."

"Protect her from what? She's got nothing but family and old friends here."

"Just protect her, in general. I knew coming home was going to be hard for her."

I slam the door behind me as I come into the kitchen and both of these full-grown men turn toward me looking like they just got caught by Mom. Raising my hand to my brother's face I let him know, "Not now," before moving onto my fiancé, "What are you doing here?"

Colby shifts back an forth on his feet, looking guilty, "It just didn't feel right letting you deal with all this alone."

I silence my brother with just a look and he sort of smiles and puts his head down, "Colby, will you meet me out back. I just need a minute with Shane."

33

"Absolutely," he says as he lays a gentle kiss on my cheek and walks out the back door.

Turning on my sibling I ask, "Why did you want me to go to the nursing home so early?"

He looks sheepishly down at his own feet, "I told you, parking."

"Bullshit. There were about four cars in the parking lot. You wanted me to run into a blast from my past, didn't you?"

His face blazes red knowing I've caught him, "Did you?"

I can't even look at him. This is going to have to wait or I might kill him, "Do you still have your four-wheelers?" He nods. "Can I take them out for a while?"

"You only need one four-wheeler for one person."

"One for me and one for Colby since I clearly can't leave him alone here with you."

"I'm sorry, my vehicles won't run for narcissistic assholes."

My eye-roll is so exaggerated that Shane can probably hear it as well as he can see it.

"Yes, you can take them..." His expression is full of melancholy, "You look just like Mom when you make that face, by the way."

That old familiar ache pops up in my gut and I want more than anything to see her face again. Shane and I share a bittersweet smile that calms me for just a moment as I grab the keys and slip out the back screen door. I pause a moment with my hand on the door. This is where she measured our heights for the 16 years we had her. My hand runs down the crudely drawn lines and seeing her handwriting reminds me of yet another reason I didn't want to come home. This is all just too much. I'm angry. I'm heartbroken all over again. I'm just overwhelmed.

Seeing Colby standing on the porch I grew up on, I just want to erase all the bad here and go back to the future he and I are building together. I know who this man is inside. I know the generous, kind spirit living inside him. I want to let go of all this that's been holding me back, all of this still somehow holding me here. It's like my life has been on pause for the last decade and I'm just exhausted from holding it all in place. I'm ready to move again.

Those good intentions propel me into a deep kiss with the man I've promised to marry. I press myself into him with such intensity that I think we might morph into one being. His soft lips moan against mine and he holds me so tight against him, hands tangling in my hair.

"What was that for," he asks with a breathless smile.

"Just because," I reply as I toss him a set of keys. His face brightens and he smiles that megawatt smile that earned him the nickname Golden Boy when we were all in high school together. I watch him as he walks toward the garage and sigh to myself while a cavernous pit grows in my gut.

Nothing in that kiss stirred the same kind of feelings that even just a fight with Cash brought back to life inside me. Not even close.

# 9

## I am a blessed man.

Savannah blames her father and I can't say I blame her. He was Beth's husband and he should have been watching over her so some maniac couldn't walk up and just steal her away. I couldn't have painted a better picture myself.

It's pretty comical if I'm honest. I wasted so much time and energy worrying about how to fix this whole mess and then it went and fixed itself. A few well-placed rumors later and no one was really even looking for her anymore. They all assumed her drunk of a husband got away with murder or she ran away from him before he tried. I kind of feel sorry for the guy now that everyone, including his own daughter, is shunning him. He's a pretty decent dude, but I'll let him fall on the blade for me any day.

It all worked out far better than I ever expected and I am loving this feeling of invincibility. I am truly a blessed man.

# 10

# Savannah

C olby is filling the ATV's with gas when I walk into the garage. He checks the tires, making sure they aren't flat. He's always taking care of me. I love that about him mostly because I haven't always been that great at taking care of myself. When he wandered back into my life I was in an incredibly low place. I was alone and falling apart. I needed someone to walk in and fix me and he did that. For the most part anyway. I'm better than I was then and I owe him the biggest debt of gratitude for that, but right here, at this moment... I just don't have anything but anger in me.

"What are you doing here?" I blast at him across the empty space between us.

He jumps then stares blankly at me, "I'm getting them ready to go..."

"Not here, right this second, in this garage. Here. Home. In the town you claim to want nothing to do with. Why?"

"I told you, I didn't feel right letting you deal with all this alone."

"And I told you that I wanted to come alone. I explicitly told you to stay there," I am boiling over with rage now and he seems shocked to see it. I don't really get angry with Colby. Annoyed, yes, but he always seems to be able to talk me down before I can really fight with him. This doesn't happen in our normal day to day life.

He stops what he's doing now and fully faces me, "I just wanted to be here for you." His big brown eyes would usually swallow up all my emotions right now, but not today.

"Sometimes I need to be there for myself."

My words seem to knock him off-kilter and I see a flash of something foreign in his face, but only for the briefest moment. Within an instant, it's gone. I think he's going to yell back for a moment too, but he simply steps back and gestures for me to take the four-wheeler he was prepping before climbing onto his own. I guess we aren't talking now so I mount mine in silence.

I turn the key and hear the growl of the machine between my legs coming to life. The exhaust smell and rough vibrations are intoxicating. They make me feel brave and dehydrated for adventure. I need to do something wild to fill this ache inside me. I think Colby is trying to talk to me, but I'll never know for sure because before he can get a word through my consciousness I am flying out of the garage and into the wild surrounding the neighborhood.

These woods are full of as many memories as the rest of my hometown. All the nights I snuck out to help Cash steam up the windows of his car. The nights we sat on that overturned tree and he held me while I cried and screamed for my mother. The walks we took down the trails planning the future we were going to build together before it all went up in flames. Being here and feeling it all in this place again makes my heart feel brand new. It makes me want to put it all on the line to feel the hurt all

38

over again. I can feel an echo of how blissfully wonderful it had been before it wasn't. I have to create a new path. I have to find a new uncharted way to go or I'm going to make all the same stupid mistakes all over again. I need to face it all from a new perspective that hasn't been a part of me before so I can find a new way to be whole and full.

Just like that, without a second thought, I turn the four-wheeler and take off into the untamed wilderness off the well-worn path. Crashing through the brush I feel the sting of branches whacking against my legs and think I might hear Colby calling my name over the snaps and pops of my off-road adventure, but I refuse to stop. The further I make it into the thick of the trees, the more frenzied I feel. It's like there is a war going on with my need to put space between everything I've known and my desire to hold it all as close to me as possible. I want both. I don't know which I want more or how to make it all work in my life without going insane. The path I'm carving out seems to get rougher with each passing second but I push on like a crazy person, just desparetly seeking something that will make it all make sense. Do I have a death wish? It would appear so, but then it all just stops.

I come to a complete halt as one of my back wheels drops down into a hole, lifting the front off the ground completely. My whole frame feels rattled and without the wind whooshing by me, I can hear my own panicked breathing. I didn't even realize my breath was escaping in loud, harsh gusts. I can hear Colby yelling my name. I can hear the echo of my past chasing after me. I feel like my world is spinning out of control and I close my eyes and cover my ears to try and block it all out.

Before I know what's happening, Colby is on me, checking me for injuries and all-around fretting over my mental and physical state. "Have you lost your mind," he says once he sees I'm perfectly fine and unhurt. "What the fuck was that, babe?"

"I... I don't know. I just... wanted to see something new," I manage to squeak out.

"Well, you definitely did that. I'm sure your brother will find a way to make this my fault..."

The jab at my brother makes me mad for a second, but I know he's right.

He stares at me seriously and shakes my shoulders a bit to bring me back to the right now, "You could have been killed, Savannah. Why would you be so stupid?"

His angry words hurt, but his face betrays the fear and pain I've just put in him. I feel awful. I sheepishly climb down from the mess I've made while he surveys the whole situation. I chew on my lip as I see the full extent of what I've done. The machine is twisted and bent at odd angles that don't look natural. Shane is going to kill me. I can't even look anymore. I think I broke my brother's toy.

I look everywhere but at the wrecked vehicle as Colby talks his way through how to fix it or at least get us unstuck, "Is it broken... I don't see anything.... well, I guess right there... but that looks minor... I think if I..."

I'm trying my hardest to let his voice become just background noise. I have so many thoughts just tumbling around in here and I think my head might explode if I let anything else thru. I let my eyes wander to take in our surroundings, seeking out simple distraction, and then suddenly my eyes settle on something bright white against the brown scattered leaves of the forest floor. Just yards from where we stand, it looks like porcelain white fingers peeking out of the cluttered blanket of fall on the ground. I'm grounded to the spot.

I can't tear my eyes away from those delicate little structures of flesh, "Colby, stop talking." My voice sounds so cold and far away. I start walking towards the glowing white skin as if I have no control over my own movement. It's almost as if a tether is drawing me to the spot. Slow measured steps carry me through the dry crunching leaves and then I see her, frozen in time.

I can't move, breathe, or speak. I can only stare into the cold, lifeless face staring back at me with unblinking eyes. Not even the thud of Colby's approaching boots smashing through the fragile leaves is enough to bring me out of her hold on me.

"What is it, babe? Oh, god."

Colby is frozen now too, staring at the corpse at our feet. Nude, she is laid there on the dirt floor of this patch of trees, her porcelain skin hidden by nothing but a thin layer of autumn's fallen leaves. Her face is petite and serene. You would think she was a painting if you didn't notice the busy crawl of insects already working to break her body down into decay. They tunnel through the tangle of her brown hair and crisscross paths across her pale skin. All the while her hazel eyes gaze up at us in a blank stare.

"Holy shit, Savannah. We have to call someone."

Colby is a chaotic mess all around me. Running his hands through his hair and frantically pacing, he searches for his cell phone. He is doing everything a normal person would but not me. I'm just standing, transfixed.

As I stare into her vacant eyes, I can only see myself. In every curve of her body, I see me. She looks just like me.

While my being cannot move, my mind races through a million thoughts and my matching greenish-brown eyes take in every detail. I'm searching for, craving, one thing to set us apart. There has to be something. This has to be a cruel

41

coincidence. I am staring at the deep marks of strangulation around her neck when a swift breeze shifts the leaves sheltering her body. That's when I see it.

There on the soft skin beside the bone of her hip is a tattoo still fresh and tender. A tiny heart-shaped lock wrapped in soft twirling ivy. Just like mine.

I can't breathe anymore. My whole body is falling to pieces. I can't stand. That tattoo meant so much to me at one point in my life. As everything starts to go black all I can see is the face of the man who wears the key to that lock forever etched into his body.

Cash.

# 11

# The Tattoo

S o many people talk about the addictive sting of a tattoo being etched onto your skin forever. Turns out I hate it. There is no control for me. I have to just sit here and let this inked up biker looking dude named Chewey drag a needle across my flesh. It's bullshit. I don't know why anyone enjoys doing this. She is the only reason I am doing this and I will never be doing it again.

Who am I kidding? If she ever asked me to get another tattoo we all know I would be back in this chair letting Chewey mutilate me again. To hell with it. Maybe I'll just teach myself to do it on my own. It couldn't be that hard, could it? At least then I can control what's happening because this bullshit is stupid.

Just keep chanting, it's all for her... it's always for her.

I can't even explain the hold she has on me. She was always kind to me in a real way, even when everyone else only faked it, but something else... I don't just love her. I need her. She's my oxygen. My world goes dark without her in it.

Right now she is not herself. I know that's my fault. I'm just hoping someday this gesture will mean something to her and she'll understand I didn't mean to hurt her. All of this has always been for her.

# 12

# Savannah

Colby asked me about my tattoo the first time we had sex. I felt that old familiar pang of heartbreak with his questions, realizing this was the first person to ever see it aside from Cash. I fed him some line about getting it after the breakup as a reminder to wait for the guy who held the key. We both laughed, he fell asleep with his arm around me, and I wept in his bed. I remember waking up the next morning with red, tired eyes and feeling the emptiness almost swallow me up.

That's how I feel now as the black begins to clear. It feels like it was all a dream until I open my eyes and see the dark woods still surrounding me. As my eyes flutter open everything around me comes into focus. Colby is looming over me calling my name.

"Savannah! Wake up, Savannah! The police are on their way!"

I just stare at him, not knowing what to say or do.

"Savannah... Are you with me?"

I manage a feeble nod, but I'm not sure how reassuring it

is. All the color in his face has drained away and he is clearly frightened. Who wouldn't be? We just found a dead body and I just fainted like a 1950's housewife. Who even does that?

I turn my head, laying my cheek against the cool damp ground, and she's right there just a foot away from me. Her life has been stolen. For the briefest of moments, it feels like I'm looking into my future. Something deep down inside me feels like I am meant to be laying here just like she is. Not taking my eyes off her face, I finally find my voice, "She's me."

"What? Babe, relax. You're still just a little woozy," he responds with entirely too much calm.

Spinning my gaze back to this man I've agreed to make my husband, I can't believe the look of pitiful disbelief on his face. He really doesn't see it? How? I push myself off the ground and point to the body, "Colby, look at her! She's me! Everything about her is me!" I can hear the hysteria building in my voice, "For Christ's sake, she even has my tattoo!"

Colby is quiet and takes a longer look at the girl before us. I can see his wheels turning. As he runs his hands through his hair, I can tell he is at a loss for words, but I don't think it will play out in my favor. He has that look he gets when he doesn't know how to let me down easy, like he thinks I'm crazy and I'm in need of being handled. I know what he's going to say before the words are even out of his mouth.

"She does look similar to you," he says in defeat, "but so do a lot of girls. It's a coincidence. You told me yourself that you picked that tattoo off the wall in some shady tattoo shop. It's probably on every other woman from here to Texas. Don't get yourself so worked up. We just walked into an ugly situation. You just need to calm down."

Those words, calm down. They infuriate me in spectacular

ways. The rational side of me wants to believe him, but every other piece of me wants to tell him where he can shove his calm down. Police sirens wailing in the distance bring me down just enough to save him from my words, but the look I swing across the space between us is enough to get him all flustered. Good. Let him sweat it out.

As I sit on the cold rocks I wrecked in the middle of, I can feel the cavernous gap I'm creating between myself and my lover. It's not just physical, my mind is shutting him off until he can find his way to seeing things my way. I know it sounds selfish as soon as I realize I'm thinking it, but this situation is exceptional. Sticking to what I believe might mean the difference between survival and being the next body.

I am turning over all the thoughts and theories running rampant through my mind when I see the red and blue flashes of police cars shining through the trees up the hill from us. My stomach twists and tightens thinking about the officers that are going to come walking down that hill. Letting someone else join this scene will cement it in reality. I can't pretend it away if everyone knows it happened. I look at this poor girl and wonder what her last moments were like. A single word brings me out of my daze.

"Vannah?"

"Cash," I whisper under my breath without raising my head. He has always been the one there for me through every hard thing I have ever encountered except losing him. Having him here for this hard moment too makes the sobs inside me want to finally rise to the surface. This poor girl's tragedy hits me like a freight train but I control the violent waves of emotion coursing through me.

Colby sees me struggling and puts aside our differences as

he rushes to my side. A flood of guilt leaves me drowning as I find myself wishing it was Cash holding me tight instead. I am a horrifyingly awful person. I make eye contact with Cash over Colby's shoulder and hate how hard his face has become. I push Colby back, "I'm fine. Really. I just need a minute."

As the two men now face each other, I can see their contempt for one another between them. They were friends once upon a time and now all of that has somehow melted away into bitter hate.

Cash shakes his head, "Don't you just look perfect next to her? I should have known..."

Before Colby can respond, I climb down off the rocks, "She's over here. I'll show you."

I lead Cash toward the young girl and say nothing. The scene needs no words. He gasps when he sees her splayed out before us. Looking at me and then back at the body he says, "Uncanny resemblance, right?" He squats over the body and looks closely at the ink carved into her skin and then stares back at me, incredulous.

I know my eyes are full of fear as I nod my head in agreement. He gets it.

Cash stands abruptly and motions the rest of the police crew over to where we stand before directing me back away from it all. Another officer, a young woman, is already talking to Colby as we approach them.

She turns to me, way to cheery to be working a serious crime scene right now, "We can talk here, Mrs. Adams-"

Cash and I both cut her off, "It's Miss Raymore." Colby scowls.

"Oh, of course. Miss Raymore, we need to ask some questions about what happened here today. We can talk here if you would rather or we can take you to the police station. It might be a little warmer and you can take a minute to collect yourself if you decide to go to the station."

Cash gently places a hand on my shoulder sending sparks through my body, "I really think going in might be for the best. I want you safe, okay?"

I nod as Colby interjects, "Not your call, man."

I stop Colby with a pleading look, "I think going to the station would be good," I reply shaking off the cold chill that has claimed me and settled in my bones.

"I'll have someone take you in, Vannah. I prefer you have an officer with you," Cash assures me at once.

Colby counters, "I can drive you there. You're not in any trouble. You can go at your own pace and without official escort." The last bit comes with air quotes and is drenched in sarcasm.

With a big sigh and a gentle hand on his chest, I let him down as gently as possible, "I really would like just a little solitude to process everything right now. You probably need that too."

He looks so sad and rejected so I place a kiss on his cheek and whisper, "I love you," before climbing the tall hill to the higher ground where the police cruisers are parked. Once at the top of the hill, a young officer places me in the backseat of an SUV police cruiser. When the doors are closed I let the now muffled noise float away as the silence of the car wraps its arms around me. Somehow I even manage to hold my composure as Cash climbs into the driver seat. Colby would not be okay with this. I assume that's why Cash chose to do it.

"Are you okay?" he asks.

"Yeah, I'm fine."

He eyes me skeptically from the rearview mirror as he begins to drive us away from this whole mess. We ride in silence for a while until I accidentally let a muffled sob escape, shattering the quiet. I nearly bite through my lip trying to retain control, but I can feel his eyes burning into me from the rearview mirror again. It seems I am nothing but tears in the last 24 hours and I hate it.

Fluidly, without any hesitation, he pulls the car to the side of the road and turns to face me, "It will always be okay for you to let go with me. I don't care how many years it's been or where we are in life or what stupid fight we had that morning, I will always be a safe place for you."

Just like that, it all pours out of me. That poor girl. She was so young. Who was she? Who is looking for her? Does she have a best friend, a brother or sister, a lover? Why the tattoo? How are we connected? Did she suffer? Will someone want to give her a pretty headstone and bring flowers to her as I did for my mother's empty grave? All these questions whiz and fly through my mind matching the urgency of my cries.

The whole time, Cash just sits quietly and lets me have my moment. We've been here before. He knows the kind of space I need and when I'm ready to be put back together. He also seems to understand that fixing me isn't his responsibility anymore. He sits solemnly on the other side of the plexiglass divider and gazes down to his lap while he lets me cry. As my sobs grow quieter and less frequent, he gives me a sad smile.

"Better?"

I nod silently and give him the smallest of smiles as well. Just like that he puts the car in drive again and pulls away into traffic.

"Thank you," I say as I begin to feel somewhat functional again.

"Anytime, Vannah," he says with a melancholy undertone to

his voice, "Anytime."

* * *

Somehow the police station interrogation room feels colder and more hopeless than the crime scene I just left. Cracked tile floors, that are probably leaking asbestos into every breath I take, reflect the flickering fluorescents, making me wonder if anyone has ever had a seizure in here. The only thing that could break their fall is this heavy, cold, metal table bolted to the floor. If they're lucky, the hard impact might just put them out of their misery. It would have to be better than staying in this room that smells like broken dreams and not enough personal hygiene. It's also about 20 below in here too and it makes me fidgety in an effort to create warmth. No wonder all those people in these rooms on Dateline look guilty as sin. I'm beginning to understand the gimmick.

With a burst of sounds, the important looking bald man from this morning enters the room with a file full of paperwork. I've already talked to one officer about what happened. What could this one possibly want?

"Evening, Miss Raymore."

He extends his hand to me and then places a picture on the table of a young girl. She is nothing more than a child, but her brown hair, hazel eyes, and soft white skin give her away. She is the girl in the woods. I have no doubt, "It's her. That's her."

"We thought it might be. We're having dental records checked but thought asking you might be faster."

"What's her name? Who is she?"

"Her name is Seraphina. She's been missing for about six months."

"That's awful. Does her family know she's been found?"

"Oh, there is no family to notify. She has been in the system since she was an infant. We honestly thought she was just a runaway. She may still be. Just a troubled girl that fell into a bad situation."

I bring my hands to my face and cover my mouth to hold in my words. The way he speaks of her does not sit well with me at all. Just because she didn't grow up with a family does not mean she has no value. She was a person.

"Miss Raymore, did you know her at all?"

The way he asks me makes me uncomfortable, "No, I don't even live here anymore. She would have been just a toddler when I left. We just found her."

"Officer Perez feels like she kind of bears are resemblance to you." He takes a long look at her photo, "I guess she does, doesn't she?"

"Yes! She does! We even have the same tattoo in the same place! I've been trying to tell people that all night and everyone acts like I'm crazy!"

"No, no. I see it too. What I'm thinking though, is that it is a strange coincidence, don't you think? You would just happen to be the one who finds a dead body that looks just like you?"

I don't even honor this with a response. The insinuation is insulting, "There's a padlock on her hip. I have the exact same one in the exact same place."

He ignores me as well as he continues on his path of questioning, "Did you guys move her body at all? Maybe roll her over or anything?"

"Oh God, no. We didn't touch her. We saw her in the leaves and then immediately called 911."

"What would you say if I told you that we found something

of yours under the body?"

Fear snarls through me like icy fingertips tightening around my torso. Having a feeling, a hunch, is different than having confirmation. My breathing shallow and caught in my throat, I answer, "I would be even more terrified than I already am."

As I squeak the words out he throws an evidence bag onto the table in front of me, "Do you recognize this?"

My mouth drops open and I reach for the bag with trembling fingers. Inside is a single photograph. The edges are worn and yellowed with age, but I would recognize it anywhere. I was 14 when it was taken. I spent that whole summer babysitting to earn money for this new outfit and haircut for school pictures. I had been so proud to sit in front of that Lifetouch photographer and smile my biggest smile. My mom carried it with her always because she said it was the most me picture she had ever seen. It disappeared right along with her. My eyes grow misty as I respond, "I haven't seen this in years."

"Turn it over," he instructs.

I slowly flip the bag over and see, written in my mom's neat script:

Savannah, 14

8th grade

My heart gives a tremendous squeeze to see her familiar handwriting again, but just below it are heavy-handed block letters:

I WOULD HAVE KEPT HER IF I'D KNOWN SHE WOULD LOOK LIKE YOU

"What does this mean?" I ask.

"We were hoping you could give us some insight into that."

My mind is reeling and coming up with a million questions, but not a single answer.

Seeing my utter loss for words, the detective saves me, "From what I have heard, you haven't been home in a good long while. It gives us here a pretty sour stomach to think that the day after you come back a body turns up in what might as well be your backyard and it all looks suspiciously tied to you. Your boyfriend has an alibi that covers him until after the girl likely died. He has a work colleague that verified he was with her until after the window of opportunity. I'm willing to bet you don't. Now, if you aren't involved in this whole thing, you need to keep in mind that it appears someone might be trying to bring you into it. You are going to need to be vigilant." I numbly nod my head and let him continue. "With some of the connotations behind the new note written on that picture, we would like to run a DNA test to see if there might be a genetic link between you and the girl."

"Seraphina," I interrupt.

"What?" he questions.

"The girl. She had a name. Seraphina." His continual use of 'the girl' feels cheap and unfair.

"Oh, uh… to check for a genetic link between yourself and Seraphina," he corrects himself with red heat climbing into his cheeks. "Would you be willing to submit a sample?"

I nod again, "Yes, absolutely. Whatever you need."

Now, I think he continues to talk, but I am certain I have checked out completely. I can do nothing but turn over all the details I was just handed in this cold little room. So much significance, but still no clear answers.

Suddenly I am brought back to attention, "Did you hear me, Ms. Raymore?"

"What? Yes… no… I'm sorry. It's a lot to take in."

For the first time in our little meeting, I think I can see

compassion in his eyes, "I understand that and we are here to help if you think of anything that might aid us in the investigation once you've had a chance to process it all. They will be in to take a DNA sample soon." The detective turns to leave the room, but faces me once more, this time with remorse in his eyes, "It's my job to follow all leads and exhaust all possibilities. I have to ask the hard questions even when I don't agree with them, but I believe that you are being honest about your involvement. There isn't really enough evidence to warrant a protective detail for you so I can't, yet, do anything specific to keep you safe, but I need you to understand that you must take care of yourself right now." I nod in understanding and he adds, "Something tells me you're going have a certain member of my police force watching out for you too." With a wink, he's out the door and gone.

* * *

The lab technician is a woman about my age and she is professional with the entire process. She explains how it will work and thanks me for my cooperation. The cheek swab is simple and quick, but I am still overwhelmed by a queasiness bubbling up my throat. I just need to leave this room. I just need to breathe. As soon as she finishes her job and gives me the okay to leave, I bound from the room. I'm sure that doesn't look suspicious at all...

I make it to the bathroom as quickly as I can and rush to the sink splashing water on my face. I reevaluate everything I just learned. They aren't sure this all has anything to do with me and are sure that it does all at the same time. I'm so profoundly frustrated.

Flinging my paper towels in the trash, I yank the door open and head back out into the hall. Above all the normal precinct noise level, I hear the voice I know so well. Sneaking up, I see him standing there with his back to me in the break room across the hall. Suddenly my heart beats a little faster and I find myself walking to the room just to be there with him for a moment, craving the comfort of his presence.

I truly have a problem.

Cash is distracted in conversation with another officer and doesn't hear me come in. I take a minute to take it all in. Seeing the shape of his body and the way he uses his hands takes me back in time. He has not changed at all. I'm so absorbed in my study of this man that I bump my body into the water cooler and send it into a gurgling frenzy. He glances over his shoulder at me and laughs a little as the other officer excuses himself.

"I didn't realize you were done in there yet. I was about to bring you some coffee. I figured you could use it."

I glance down at the counter in front of him and see two cups of coffee, one starkly lighter in color than the other. He hands me the lighter of the two.

"No sugar, mostly creamer, with a splash of coffee," he tells me with a smirk as he walks to the doorway to leave. He hesitates for a moment as I take a delightful sip of my perfect cup of coffee and gives me a proud nod when he sees the delight on my face.

"Cash, wait," I call as he walks out. He turns to face me again and I want to apologize for our argument this morning. I want to tell him I want a do-over. I want to thank him for his help today. I want to say a million things, but I don't know how to make any of it come out. Instead, I simply say, "It's perfect. Thank you."

Seeming to be thinking through what he wants to do next, Cash pauses at the door before slowly walking back across the room to me. He brings himself so close that I can't breathe for a moment. He brings his face down to mine and I can feel the rush of heat to my face as I think, just for a moment, that he is going to press his lips to mine. At the last second, he turns his head and whispers in my ear instead. His voice is hot and breathy in my ear, "Vanna, I will always know what you like."

Just like that, he's gone and I feel like my whole body might burst into flames. I take a hard swallow from my cup and the strong coffee taste gives me the jolt of self-awareness I needed. While I stand here fantasizing about a man that I don't belong to anymore, I have neglected to take into account his connection to the body, to Seraphina. She may be wearing my tattoo on her body, but Cash wears the match and he is the only person on the planet, aside from myself, that knows it's deep meaning. If that bit of information connects me to a horrific crime, shouldn't it connect Cash as well?

With a hard swallow, I let the realization sink in that my ex-lover may not be who I thought he was.

# 13

## Double Life

L iving a double life is the greatest exercise of wit and agility that I could ever imagine existing in the world. It wears me out, but it's satisfying as hell.

I can spend all night breaking every moral code imaginable then spend the next day carrying groceries home for little old ladies and walking my mom to the first row in church. Everyone loves me. They think I'm a good guy. They smile and wave at me when I meet them on the sidewalk. They trust me alone with their wives and sisters.

The psychology of it all is so interesting. No one really takes the time to look below the surface. As long as you give them the pretty smile and say all the right things, they just don't care to know what's under your shiny exterior. Everything is an illusion, but that's okay because the illusion is comfortable. It doesn't make them question everything they thought they knew about the world. People don't want to know the truth if it makes them uncomfortable. It doesn't matter that I have fantasized about 100 different ways I could end their life, as long as I hide that part of me deep down inside. As long as I lock it up with a smile and polite conversation.

And then I get to have the best of both worlds. I get to hear how wonderful I am, how bright my future is. I get to be the hero of everyday life, but I also get to be the monster. I have found the way to balance societal expectations and true desires. All of those famous killers and criminals gave into their needs, but they got caught because they didn't know how to play the part of the alter ego. That's the secret.

Do that and they will never question you.

# 14

# Savannah

When an officer drops me off at Shane's house, I am beyond belief excited to see no one home. I need a hot shower to wash my fears away and I need a cold shower to wash off the completely inappropriate frenzy that Cash sent my hormones into. I opt for the cold shower first and step into the stream of water before it has any time to warm up. The ice-cold droplets hit my skin in sharp stings of pain, but I feel like I've earned the punishment. The fact that I still let Cash do to me what he does, and especially when I now have suspicions of him swirling in my mind, is disgusting.

Slowly heat sneaks into the stream of water falling down my skin and I lean into its comfort. Why did I come back? Why? Colby and I were doing fine. We were building a life. I should have had no issues in moving forward with that. My brother though. If I hadn't come back I wouldn't have him back. Silver linings. Although he's probably wishing his wayward sister hadn't brought all this drama to his otherwise quiet doorstep.

I let the water roll down my skin until the heat recedes back to chilling cold once again. I let it soak me and drown out my shrieking thoughts. I let it soothe me until I feel human again. I get out of the shower a new woman.

Walking down the stairs, toweling off my wet hair, I think I have some refreshed perspective. I can see and think a little more clearly. I'm building a plan and strategy to approaching all my world's problems. The house is still and calm and quiet. I can go stand in the kitchen, eat a snack, drink a beer, and fix everything I need to figure out. It's amazing what a nice long shower can do for a girl. I almost even have a spring in my step as I round the corner into my mom's old eat-in kitchen, but I freeze and feel all of my confidence drain out of me as I peer at the scene in front of me.

Sitting around my mother's kitchen table are Colby, Shane, and Cash, all silently eyeing each other from across the table. The air is thick with awkwardness... Shane is directly in the middle and as his wide eyes make contact with mine, he is silently mouthing, help me.

I want to laugh at this but I'm afraid of what might happen if I break the silence. Instead, I just walk on past the gathering like I can't even see it. Just like that, my brother joins me on the other side of the swinging door to the dining room.

"Why would you leave them alone in there," I ask.

"Why would you leave me alone in there with them," he asks in answer.

"Touché," I say with a nod. "What are they both doing here," I whisper.

"You are why Golden Boy is here... Cash is here because he's here almost every night. You've been gone for a long time."

"So, what? You and Cash are besties now," I ask with a raised eyebrow. I can never remember a time that my big brother ever liked my boyfriend growing up. At all.

"A lot changes when you disappear for a decade, Savvy." I feel elicit shame at his words and he can see it written all over my face. "I didn't mean that to be a dick. It's just true. Cash is a really good dude and he's a good friend. He comes over for drinks when it's been a rough day and today has been an especially bad one."

"Yeah, I get it. I'm glad you're there for each other."

As we both prepare to apologize for all the uncertainty of our relationship, we hear shouts from the kitchen. We enter the room and Cash is coming across the table at a Colby that appears completely shocked, but now ready to fight. I rush to hold Colby back. Shane rushes to get between the two.

"Cash, he's not worth it, buddy," Shane exclaims, shaking his friend's shoulders.

"Fuck you, asswad," Colby throws in and makes me want to punch him. I should want to stand up for Colby, but that's my brother.

"Colby! Stop it," I command while shoving him back down into his chair.

"Cash, let's head to the bar. We'll walk. You can calm down."

Cash and I make eye contact and his eyes are pleading, "Why are you with this piece of trash? Why don't you see what you're worth?"

I have no words to respond. I simply stare back, trying to understand what just happened here.

Shane quickly rushes Cash out the door, "I told you, bud. This guy isn't worth your time. Let's go."

Words fly at my brother, "You're a piece of shit, Shane! Fuck you," as Colby jerks himself out of my grasp.

When I face him again and see his anger firing directly at my brother, I am livid. This whole thing is ridiculous and they are acting like children, "What the hell was that Colby?" The glare he gives me could kill but he says nothing, "You can't talk to my brother like that. Seriously. I just got him back."

He spins on me and is in my face, breathing fury into my lungs, "But your brother can talk to me like that?"

I could say his reaction has me stunned silent because I've never seen him like this, but I honestly just don't know what to say. He's right. It's such a double standard, but at the end of the day, Shane is my brother.

"For fuck's sake, babe. I get he's your brother, but where does that leave me? Who am I to you?"

"You know I love you, Colby."

"Do you? Do you really though? Since I've been here, you want nothing but to run even farther away from me. Shane hates me because I'm not Cash, which is ironic considering he hated him before we left, and you look at Cash like you have never looked at me. I get that they were both all you had when we were kids, but where were they for all the years I've taken care of you? Where have they been while I worked my ass off to build something better than this fucking town for you? Were they there when you were lost and scared? Were they? When someone broke in and tried to take everything you had to give? Did they hold you while you cried that night? No. It was me. I am all you have had for the last 5 years. They left you when you needed them, but I've been here."

I can do nothing but stare at him in silence. He's right. He's completely right, well, mostly right, but I am the only one that did any leaving. There are no words that I can force out of me in agreement because the more I mull it over... I feel so conflicted about the whole thing.

He shakes his head in disappointment, running his hands

through his hair as he paces the kitchen erratically, "I need to go for a run."

My silence has told him everything he needs to know and he stomps upstairs to change his clothes. I start to pursue him, but he stops me with a glare. It takes him just minutes to return in his running clothes. He won't even look at me as he walks past and slams the door on his way out. I have this overwhelming feeling that says I'm not sure if he'll come back. I can't say I blame him.

The stillness of the house in his absence feels so different than the stillness when I got home this afternoon. Where it was freeing and welcoming, it is now cold and full of uncertainty. Did I just use my silence to end my relationship? Is it wrong that I'm not sad about it?

It's a strange feeling to be both horribly upset and kind of okay with it all at once. It gives me an uneasy twisting in my belly. On the one hand, if he leaves I'll be fine. I'll survive. It won't crush my world. I've lived through far worse. On the other hand, I don't know if I would ever forgive myself. That would be the agony. He is right. He is 100% right. I owe him so much better than I've ever given him. I do love him. I do care about him, but before him I had already lost so much that I just don't have a lot left to give him.

As my mind wanders to my mom, my body has wandered to the room where she laid her head down to sleep for as long as we had her. Shane and I promised each other that as long as we had any control over this house, her space would always be left exactly the same. We would never erase her from this place and I smile to see he kept the pact. I walk to the bed that I used to crawl into when I had a bad dream. I run my hands along the cool quilt that I watched her stitch together with her own hands. When I sit on the edge of the bed, I can almost still see a younger version of myself being chased through this very doorway, giggling like crazy as Mom would pick me up and swing me onto the bed. I see myself as a barely teenager, laying here telling her about the boy I loved. Maybe that's why he is so hard to let go, he is still some shred of a tie to my mom. She loved him too, like one of her own.

I lay my body out across her bed and let my tears fall for her. I have cried more tears since being home than I have cried in the last 5 years altogether. It's like a huge damn was holding them all in and it has suddenly come crashing down. Nuzzling in, I find that her pillow somehow still smells like her. Maybe I just want it to, but I breathe it in until my lungs are full of her essence anyway. I miss her so much.

At least I had her for a while. Seraphina was never lucky enough to have a mother at all. The thought makes me wish I could have known her. I wish I could have somehow given her a piece of the love my mother gave me. I wish I could have held her when she was sad and celebrated with her when she felt joy. Maybe then her circumstances could have been different. Maybe that was all she needed in her life to save her, just to have people that loved her enough to look out for her. Maybe that's all any of us really need.

* * *

I don't even realize I've fallen asleep until the blaring explosion of my obnoxious ringtone jerks me back to life. It's Colby calling. I can tell by the song coming out of my phone. I should answer, but I am so warm in my mother's bed and I just don't want to fight anymore tonight. I want to keep letting the memory of her hold me tight. I let the call go to voicemail.

Expecting to hear my chime for a new message, I instead hear my ringtone again immediately. Ugh... I just want to throw the pillows over my head and disappear. A brief pause and the trilling tones of my phone again. The sleepy fog finally starts to subside and I realize he's calling again for the fourth time now. Fear grasps ahold of me and I scramble to find my phone hidden in the folds of my mom's quilt.

"Colby? Hello?"

"Savannah? God, fuck..." his voice is rough and strained.

"Colby are you okay?" Fear grips my insides and I hate myself for not picking up more quickly or being more concerned when he left so upset.

"Holy hell... this guy, he came out of nowhere... Fuck, my head..."

"Where are you? Did you call 911? What happened?"

"Can you just come get me? I feel kind of fuzzy..." he slurs almost incoherently.

"Where are you???"

"Oh, God... um... South Commerce I think. Just down the road from the school."

"I'm on my way! Stay where you are." I grab my keys and hurl myself out the door.

# 15

## Killing is easy.

K illing someone is the easy part. Living with them is hard. Letting them live is hard.

Ending a life erases their presence. It alleviates the pain of having to deal with their needs and cries, their useless oxygen stealing existence. Erasure is joyful. I take immense pleasure in ridding the world of extra bodies.

Watching this useless piece of shit taking up space in her world and not being able to just bash his brains in is maddening. Why can she not just walk away from him? I don't want to share time with him. I want him to disappear. I want to be the one to make him disappear. Unfortunately, I learned the hard way with her mommy dearest that yanking people out of her life might not be the best way to go. I broke something in her with that one so now I have to just wait this one out. Let him fade away from her as I plant lie after lie after lie all around to make her hate him.

I can only come up with so many rumors before I officially blow a fuse and just do away with him entirely. I'll never understand her draw to him. Never. She deserves so much better.

# 16

## Savannah

The last hour of my life is a complete blur. I rushed to Colby, not sure what state I would find him in. I panicked when he looked up at me from the curb he was sitting on with blood pouring down his face. Getting him in the car was a crazy struggle. He was lethargic and confused. Half of me wanted to say to hell with it and wait for an ambulance, the police needed to be called anyway, but I also knew it would end up taking longer than just doing it myself. The amount of blood was staggering and I was afraid at any moment he was going to go unconscious. We didn't have time to wait. I filled his hands with random fast food napkins from the glove box and then threw myself back into the driver's seat. I spent the entire 25-minute drive to the hospital flying down residential streets, checking to make sure he was still awake, and talking to a 911 dispatcher to make sure police were meeting us at the hospital.

When I skidded into the emergency room drop off they rushed him in like he might be on the verge of literal death. Pretty impressive for a hospital with a normal wait time of 5ish hours which had me beyond terrified. I kept wondering, had I spent the last bit of time I had with him fighting and making him feel like I don't care? Guilt was tearing at me in serious ways, but then the nurse called me back and he is okay.

Just like that, everything is fine.

His blood-stained shirt has been removed and replaced with a clean white gown and the long lines of blood streaking his face have been washed away. His face is still ashen white but he's giving me a slight smile.

I rush over and wrap my arms around him in a tight embrace. He winces a little but lets me have my moment.

"Are you okay?"

"Yeah, I will be. Cracked a rib and got a cut on my head. They said it bled a lot because head injuries always do and I was disoriented most likely from shock over what all happened."

"What did happen?"

"I don't really know for sure. I was just running along Commerce and this guy came up all dressed in black with his face covered. He didn't say anything, just bashed me over the head and ran off," he says with a shrug.

"Oh, Colby. I don't even know what to say."

Colby pauses for a moment before lowering his gaze, "Say you were right."

"What do you mean?"

"I think you called it when you said that girl is somehow tied to you." Relief floods my body. I'm not crazy. "Everything that already happened today and then I, someone directly connected with you, get attacked? It can't all be a coincidence."

"No, I don't think so either."

Reaching for my hand, he says, "At the police station, they asked me all kinds of questions about you, more about you than about what happened. How about you? Did they tell you anything?"

I start to answer but hesitate. I don't know what it is but somewhere inside I have this gnawing need to keep it all to myself, "No more than we already know, really. They were pretty evasive." I'm a terrible liar and his expression tells me he knows.

He bows his head for a moment, "I'm sorry about earlier."

"No, Colby, don't."

"Listen, I am actually sorry. I didn't mean to lose my cool like that. It's just being here again..."

"Yeah." We both know this town stirs up all the things we've tried to forget, "I'm sorry too."

He gives my hand a squeeze and as we look at each other, we know we both share a secret. This town never left us no matter how hard we tried to leave it. No matter how far we ran or how long we stayed away, everything that happened here is still inside us. It hasn't gone away, it's just been dormant, waiting for the right moment to erupt and spew its darkness over our lives again. The gravest part of this inner secret we hold inside us? We both know this time we might not survive it.

* * *

How much crap can the universe pile on in one day? Coming home from the hospital to just my brother is apparently too much to ask. I can't complain because this is his house and I am just invading it, but all the ground I made up with Colby seems to melt away into nothing as he walks into Cash going through the kitchen doorway. I can tell Colby is doing his damnedest to keep his cool, but the concerned look on Cash's face seems to draw out Colby's hate.

Placing a hand on Colby's arm, Cash says, "All differences aside, man, are you okay?"

Colby jerks his arm away and nearly snarls in Cash's face, "I'm fine."

Shane rolls his eyes, but Cash gestures that it's all good and lets it go. I feel like we're hanging out in a minefield and can't wait for Colby to retreat upstairs where we can eat our greasy takeout together in peace, but instead, he takes a seat at the kitchen counter. This gesture of acceptance towards our life and my past makes me smile at Colby. He really is a good man. This whole thing is just hard.

As I sit down next to him and begin tearing into my food, I hear a voice coming from the other room that instantly takes me back in time. All of a sudden I'm twenty again, spying around the corner as the man I thought would love me forever gives my best friend, Gabby Hernandez, a diamond ring. I can still hear her trilling voice exclaim over how much she loves it. I can still see the look of complete and total love on Cash's face as she wraps her arms around his neck.

Hearing her voice now is like feeling my heart break all over again. It feels fresh and raw. Holy shit. I really never processed any of this back then. I just crammed it down inside me, still unresolved and infected with pain. It has finally chased me down. It feels like a thousand pounds sitting on my chest. It is blisteringly hurtful and then she walks into the room. My whole world goes red when I see her face. I am full of fury instantly.

Shane smiles at Gabby as she joins us in the kitchen, "Savvy, you remember Gabby."

She smiles her biggest smile at me, but I do not return the gesture. How could he ever think I would be happy to see her?

Because I never told him, that's why. I never told anyone, ever. I have kept the events of that day to myself for all this time. I take a deep, soothing breath before I release a dripping with sarcasm answer, "Good to see you, Gabby. I'm pretty tired. I think I'll eat my dinner in my room."

"I will definitely join you," Colby says with deeply apparent relief.

Shane frowns and Gabby looks sad as Colby and I gather our things and head upstairs. I fume the entire way. How stupid could I be? I spend five minutes with Cash after ten years and I already let him in my head again. Of course, he is still with Gabby. He threw away everything we had for all those years for her. She must mean the world to him. That realization makes me even more livid. I am positive I stomp up every stair and I know I slam the bedroom door. I am shoving fries mindlessly into my mouth and staring into space with furious thoughts running through my head when Colby comes up behind me. He places a calming hand on the small of my back and plants a gentle kiss on my hair.

My body is already buzzing with angry heat and I decide to seize the moment. Turning to face him, I smash our mouths together and focus all my tension into sparking a fire between our bodies. Cash wants to parade the girl he left me for in my face, then... well, at least sex will make a great distraction.

I tangle my fingers in Colby's hair and try to push him toward the bed, but he resists and pushes me away.

"Are you trying to have revenge sex with me right now," he asks while looking furious.

The accusation slaps me in the face. I am, indeed, trying to have revenge sex with him. What the actual fuck is wrong with me? I feel all my anger drain away only to be replaced with shame. The anger seems to have skid across the floor and seeped into Colby instead. His face is red and splotchy.

"It's really never going to be me is it? It will always be him."

"Colby, I-" I want to reassure him, tell him no, he's wrong, but he cuts me off.

"Just stop. I don't even want to hear it," he says as he throws his still untouched food in the trash and climbs straight into bed.

I stand numbly watching him roll to face away from me. What is wrong with me? Why do I keep doing this to him? It's becoming more and more clear that it's time to set him free so I can't hurt him anymore. Although, it's also long past when I should let go of the past, but I can't seem to do that either.

Maybe I'm defective...

# 17

## She's Gone.

She's gone. Just like that. In the blink of an eye. Gone. She packed up everything she couldn't live without and loaded it into a cab in the middle of the night. Why would she just leave? I don't understand. I'm here and I try to give her everything I can. I watch over her to keep her safe. I bend over backward for her. I have put myself in danger for her. All for her.

I've made some mistakes but it has always been for her. I don't understand why she can't appreciate what I've done, what I've put myself through. So ungrateful. So hurtful. I honestly can't believe she would do this to me.

I don't know... Maybe some distance is good for us for now. I'm so angry with her, but I know if I hurt her, I will regret it later. I just need some time to think, to strategize. I just need to decide where to go from here. I need to figure out what comes next.

# 18

## Savannah

**E**arly morning light filters through the thin curtains but fails to shed any light on all my crazy. I haven't slept all night. I tried but did nothing except toss and turn. I have questioned everything for hours instead. Why can't I let Colby go? Why can't I just love him? Why do I still feel such a strong pull to Cash? Have I ever known who he is at all or was the person I knew just a mirage? Who was Seraphina? Why do I feel so inexplicably tied to her? Why does my mother's presence still feel so strong all around me?

Around sunrise, I finally gave up and climbed out of bed. Ever since, I have been standing in front of my mirror staring at the little lock etched into my skin. It's as if I am hoping it will morph into something entirely new, erasing my link to Seraphina and to Cash. Also, cutting Cash's tie to the lost girl in the leaves. It could free us both from so much heartache and uncertainty. Maybe if I stare long enough at the elaborate scrolling lines of the metal and twirling leaves surrounding it, maybe if I look hard enough, I will find some way to make it different... some way to wipe away the implications of its perfect replication.

The bedsprings creak behind me and I rush to drop my shirt over my inked skin as Colby comes to stand behind me. As he wraps his arms around me, I let myself lean into his warmth, so glad to find he seems to have forgiven me.

"Trying to wish that thing away?" he asks staring into my reflected eyes.

I blush at being caught, "There's just something..." I let my sentence trail off. If I share my fears, it will also mean admitting I lied.

He nuzzles my neck, "What is it, babe?"

I struggle to answer but his tender kisses on my neck make me feel both at ease and full of guilt. I lift my shirt to see it again, "It's just that it's a perfect match and no one's really ever seen it..."

"Except you, me, and Cash, " he finishes for me. I raise my eyes to meet his in the mirror, shock undoubtedly covering my face. "I'm not stupid, babe. The way you reacted when I asked you about it that first time... I kind of figured the story was a little different than you said. Not to mention I saw Cash's key years ago in the locker room when it was still fresh."

I feel terrible that he has always seen through my lies, "I'm sorry, Colby."

"Don't worry about it. We both had lives before each other. I can't be mad about something from way back then. It does make you think though, doesn't it?" He studies it for a moment and, looking like he thinks he might already know the answer, asks, "Where'd the design come from?"

Cash is a wonderful artist. Everyone who has ever known him knows it.

Neither of us speaks it out loud, but it hangs in the air between us. How does someone perfectly replicate a tattoo, in intricate detail, if they've never seen it before? It's not possible.

Wanting to lessen my fretting mind, Colby squeezes me tight and turns my body to face his, "I know you were mad, but I'm still glad I came. I just want to keep you safe." He kisses my lips sweetly and with so much love. Picking me up, he lays me down on my bed and slowly makes love to me for the first time in weeks. My mind is still not at ease and my anxiety fills my entire being, but I let him also try to fill me with his love. I'm hoping, desperately, it has the power to both heal and protect me from my past. Yet, I still feel empty.

* * *

Colby left me to go to the coffee shop in town for a while. He needed to get some work done remotely and I was fine to let him go. When he was gone I laid in bed for a while staring at the ceiling. I felt cold and empty inside. Nothing he was able to give to me was enough to fill the holes in my soul. I am beginning to think nothing ever will. The closest I may ever come is being as near to my mom as I can get. That's what brought me out into the countryside this morning. Nestled deep within the rolling hills, barely even visible if you don't know what to look for, is Lee Hill Cemetery.

Four years after mom went missing, and just weeks before I left home, she was legally declared dead. We had no body to bury, but Shane and I felt she needed a place to rest, even if only symbolically. We bought her a plot and had a memorial placed in her honor. It wasn't completed before I left so this is the very first time I have ever laid eyes on it. Perfectly manicured green grass surrounds her white marble stone reading: Beth Raina Raymore. There are fresh flowers in the vases on either side of the stone and I know Shane has been visiting her as well. I smile knowing he has been here for her.

I fall to my knees on the empty grave and run my fingers over her stone, "I miss you, Mom." I don't expect a response, but a cool breeze blows through the trees and ruffles my hair. It is just enough to help me feel like she can hear me. "Mom, I wish you were here. I am so scared and so confused. I need you here to hold my hand and tell me what to think. Mom, I am afraid Cash is someone I didn't ever think he could be. I'm afraid he's done something terrible." I heave a deep sigh and continue on to the most terrifying thought I've been churning over in my mind, "I'm afraid that I might still keep loving him anyway."

Because that is the real crux of the matter, isn't it? I fear that, even though he may have done these terrible things, I will still be drawn to him like a moth to the flame. I fear that I will get too close and get burned, that he will burn down what's left of everyone I love all because of me. My brother. Colby. I fear that I am so self-destructive and self-sabotaging that I will be the reason they both get hurt beyond repair. I'm afraid that loving me in all my selfish glory will be what breaks them.

Another breeze blows through the trees and shifts my thought process, what if it isn't him? What if my mind is twisting everything to fit something it isn't? What if I am trying to place blame where there isn't any just so that I can have answers? Why is this all happening? Why did a beautiful, young girl have to die? Why can't she still be here walking around? It's not Cash. It can't be Cash. But if it isn't him then who is it? Someone stole her life to play with me and that just isn't fair.

"Mom, please help me. I want to understand," I plead as I lay my face against her cold stone, trying to feel as close to her as possible. The wind blows once more and I relish its cold touch.

I watch as it blows leaves away from the base of Mom's vases and I catch a glimmer of color wrapped around it. My bracelet.

I feel a smile tug at the corners of my mouth as I reach out and touch the delicate beads I wore around my wrist for years. Tiny yellow and orange daisies circle around the band, framing in my favorite nickname, Vannah. Cash made it for me when we were just 12. It was my most prized possession right up until the day I left. Shane must have brought it here and left it so a little piece of me could be here too. I love that.

I tug gently at the beads, turning it to see the whole thing for the first time in so long, but something is different. As the beads with my name come across into my vision, they don't make sense. They aren't right. One by one they face me spelling out something entirely different.

S-E-R-A-P-H-I-N-A

No. No. No!

Why? This was another thing that I shared only with Cash. Of course, our whole world knew it existed, I wore it like a medal of honor, but it was only ours. Now we have yet another link between our love and the girl that had her life stolen. Half of me sees it and is sure it means Cash is guilty and only toying with me until it is my turn, the other half of me knows Cash is far too smart to leave clues that are this obvious to his own guilt.

I turn over what to do and what to think. I stare down at my mom's gravestone praying she sends me an answer.

She doesn't. I go with my gut instead.

I carefully remove the bracelet and slip it around my wrist. I carefully examine each bead before pulling my sleeve down to cover it. Looking around to make sure no one has seen my theft, I push away thoughts begging me to call the police or report it in person. I guess I have made my choice as to where my loyalties lie.

* * *

Leaving the cemetery, my only goal was to go home and find Shane. I am overjoyed to find that Colby still hasn't made it back and my brother's truck is sitting in the driveway. Shane is sitting on the couch watching college football and I walk myself directly in between him and the tv.

"Can I help you?" he asks with annoyance.

"I need you to promise me something."

He immediately looks weary at my request, "I think that's going to depend on what the promise is."

"Actually, I think it's going to be a couple promises."

He rakes his hands down his face, "What is it, Savvy?"

I take a deep breath and blow it all out for courage, "I need you to promise me that you will listen to everything I have to say and not say anything until I'm done."

He takes a long moment to think it through, but relents, "Okay, lay it on me."

"And I need you to promise me you won't tell anyone what I tell you." He says nothing but nods his head in agreement. "You swear?" Another nod and the gesture of a pinky promise from him are all I need to dump it all out on him. I join him on the couch and tell him everything. Every. Single. Thing. He listens intently as I lay it all out for him. He studies my tattoo when I tell him and acknowledges that he has seen Cash's match. He remembers the picture of me that Mom carried in her wallet. He takes in every detail of the bracelet and admits that, to the best of his memory, it is a complete replica of mine from the old days. He makes no argument and lets me tell him everything.

He waits for my permission to comment, "Well, what do you think?"

"I'm allowed to talk now?" I nod in approval. "Okay, I think it's all bullshit."

My hopes plummet and leave me feeling more vulnerable than I would like to admit, "Well, it's not. It's all true."

"No, that's not what I mean. I believe that it's true. I just don't believe for five seconds that Cash has a thing to do with it. He's not that guy. It's been a long time and I know him better than you do now. It's not him."

I close my eyes and smile because I knew this is the answer my brother would give and it's exactly what I wanted to hear. Even with all the evidence in front of him, he has faith that his friend isn't the type of person that would ever do something so horrific. I start to respond, but Colby beats me to it from where he's been listening from the doorway, "I think that is a complete cop-out bullshit line."

Shane is immediately pissed, "This guy again. Fuck off, dude."

"No, I have as much, if not more, right to take care of your sister and I think that's bullshit."

"What the fuck do you know? You haven't been around almost as long as she hasn't been around. You don't know jack shit about anybody in this town anymore."

"I know that every single piece of evidence points to your good buddy being a crazy obsessive stalker still hung up on the girl that got away and I'm not about to let her get hurt by him."

Shane is livid now and stands up to get in Colby's face, "All that evidence looks a little too perfect to me. Maybe that killer wants us all to think it's Cash because he has something to gain from Cash being gone."

82

We both know what Shane is insinuating and Colby takes the bait, "I wasn't even here when that girl died. I don't even live here anymore. You need to look a little closer to home, buddy."

They are inches from each other's faces now and I'm not about to let them tear each other apart, "Alright, enough. Shane, Colby is right." Colby's chest puffs out a little at my back up, "Colby meet me upstairs. I'll be there in a minute."

He goes without a word, but Shane turns to face me, "I don't want that piece of shit in my house anymore. You? You are welcome as long as you want. Move in if you want, but I want him out. I've never liked him and I don't trust him."

"Shane, he means well."

"Yeah. Sure. Either way, I want him out. And you need to take some time to think about what motivation he might have to be trying to scare you into thinking Cash is a bad guy." I say nothing because what is there to say? "Makes sense, doesn't it? Makes more sense than anything else so far, doesn't it? It doesn't take a genius to see how you feel about Cash and it takes even less to see how he never stopped feeling about you. Colby sees it as clear as the rest of us. He may not have been the one that killed that girl, but he sure as hell will benefit from you thinking it was Cash."

He leaves me with that and I am swimming in confusion even more than I was before.

* * *

I promised Colby I would be there in a minute, but it has been well over 2 hours before I slide into the sheets beside him. I just couldn't shut my brain off. Now, I move as slowly and silently as possible so I don't wake him. I just can't take anymore tonight.

As I burrow under the covers and try to close my eyes for much-needed sleep, Colby rolls to snuggle up next to me. He kisses my hair and rolls my body to be under his own. He begins kissing me in all the places he knows I normally like, but I put a hand to his chest to push him away. I just can't lay here and let it happen tonight. I don't have it in me.

He lifts his head and looks at me, "What's wrong, babe?"

"I just don't feel great. I think I just need some sleep." I smile at him, but it doesn't soothe his worry.

"Babe, please don't let what Shane said get in your head. You know me. You know a me that no one else does. I just want what's best for you. I want you safe. With me."

I smile and kiss him on his sweet lips to put him at ease, "I'm not. I really just don't feel good. I promise."

Colby looks uneasy, but he relents. With a soft kiss on my nose, he lays by my side and wraps me in his arms. I let him spoon me and try to let his embrace take me away to sweet sleep. It doesn't though. I spend the rest of the night staring at the empty space in front of me wondering how in the world the only two men I have ever loved in my 30 years of life are the only ones that I can possibly imagine being involved in the murder of an innocent girl.

# II

# LIVING AGAIN

*"Suddenly you're ripped into being alive. And life is pain, and life is suffering, and life is horror, but my god you're alive and it's spectacular."*
–Joseph Campbell

# 19

## Savannah

Another restless night of next to no sleep has done little for the deep dark circles under my eyes, but it has put some things into perspective for me. It is time to move forward one way or another. I felt Colby climb out of bed before the sun and with the current state of things I have to wonder if he will return at all. If he doesn't, I can't blame him. I would understand completely. I might even give him a high-five for making a good choice. If he does come back it's time for a serious conversation about where we go from here. Or rather, where we clearly aren't going. It's not okay to keep doing whatever this is that we're doing now. He deserves better than that and I need a clear head to make sense of everything going on.

I think about how the conversation might go as I pull the coffee down from the cabinet it's been in since before I can remember. It makes me feel warm inside to see how much Shane has kept the same. He and I spent so many nights in this kitchen with her, it would feel so wrong to move anything from where she had lovingly placed it all those years ago.

I hear rustling behind me as I fill the coffee pot. I look over my shoulder and see Gabby walking into the kitchen. She's here again?! I roll my eyes but decide to lean into the new leaf I'm trying to turn and grab a second mug for her.

"Good morning," she says hesitantly.

I grit my teeth but manage a kind reply, "Good morning, Gabby. Coffee?"

She smiles, "Yes, please. Your brother never drinks coffee with me in the mornings."

My brother? Something strikes me and I ask, "Did you and Cash stay here last night?"

She gives me the strangest look and shakes her head, "Um... no. Just me."

I spin around on her and my words rush out, "What is my brother to you?"

Immediately her cheeks flush red and she smiles, "I've been with Shane for years. I forget you guys haven't talked in so long. I usually stay here on nights when I'm not working."

"Huh," I say as I turn back to the coffee pot, "You and Cash didn't last long?" The words are out of me before I can stop them.

Gabby laughs hysterically in response, "Me and Cash? Hardly. No, that's never been a thing."

"You don't have to lie, Gabby. I saw you two together, back before I left..." I let the implications of that timing hang in the air between us.

She blinks a few times, staring blankly at me, "Is that why you left? You thought I was with Cash?"

Heavy silence sits between us and everything goes fuzzy from the tears filling my eyes but refusing to fall, "That wasn't the only reason." That's at least part of the truth.

Gabby's hand goes over her mouth and she looks a little teary herself, "How could you ever think I would do that to you? You were my best friend, Savvy. More like a sister."

I chew on my cheeks trying to construct my thoughts into something that makes sense. She seems so genuine, but… "Gabby, I saw you together."

She shakes her head violently, "No. You didn't. I don't know what you saw, but I have never, not ever, been with Cash. Doing that is not who I am and even if it was, Cash never wanted anything but you. He's never given me a second glance."

I had known Gabby wouldn't do that to anybody, let alone a friend, yet I had never questioned what I saw. Why had I never thought deeper than what was in front of me, never asked questions?

It wasn't just me though. There were rumors. I remember now. Whispers in the grocery store. Giggles when I walked by. People were talking about Cash playing me for a fool. Acquaintances warned me to watch out for my heart. Why did I just now remember all that? Where did that chunk of memory go until this moment? Was I blocking it? Did it even happen or am I just trying to fill in holes?

Suddenly I'm rethinking every decision I've made since that day and feeling completely insane, but no. I'm not crazy. I know I saw something, maybe it wasn't Gabby… no, it was definitely her. Spinning out in my own mind, I rationalize to her, "He had jewelry. You hugged him. The way he looked at you…"

She sits thoughtfully for a moment and then a light bulb clicks on over Gabby's head, "Were we at the Mexican place in Gainesville?" I nod. "We went there so we would know you wouldn't see us and we could make plans for how he was going to surprise you. The jewelry was for you, Savvy. He wanted to show me to make sure I thought you would love it, as if there was any doubt. I hugged him because I was excited. It was a ring. Any love you saw in his face was because he thought he was going to marry you." All the air has left my lungs. I broke my own heart and for no reason. Gabby can see the pain written all over my face, "Oh honey. I didn't mean to make you sad." She embraces me and my floodgates open. So many tears. I'm so tired of crying!

"Why not hurt me?" I ask. "I've been so unfair to you."

Taking my face in her hands she reassures me, "People make mistakes. It was 10 years ago. Forgive and forget."

Smiling a little now, I put my hands on her face as well and mirror her, "Thank you."

"What is happening in here," Shane calls from the doorway, looking a little afraid to come in.

Gabby and I both laugh as we wipe away each other's tears and hug, "We're just getting reacquainted," I say and Shane's smile is enough to make my whole day.

I know there is more to why I took what I saw back then the way that I did. I know in my bones there is a reason why I ran without even thinking. I cannot for the life of me remember what it was, and I will figure it out, but for now, it can wait. Now I just want to welcome these two back into my life without any hesitation or reservations. Right now I just want my family back.

Gabby squeezes my hand, "This handsome brother of yours is pretty awesome, Savvy."

I make a gagging noise and Shane says, "Watch it," before leaving us in the kitchen for much-needed girl talk. I haven't had a girlfriend since Gabby.

"I'm glad I saw you this morning, Savvy. I wanted to tell you that I am so sorry about what happened on Saturday. I can't imagine how frightening that must have been. Sera was an awesome girl."

I can't hide my surprise, "You knew her?"

Gabby waves me off, "Not personally or anything, just from the hospital. I'm an ER nurse and I saw her on and off through the years. She didn't really have a home, she was a system kid, so she came to us for all kinds of stuff. I really enjoyed her."

"I can't get her out of my head. From what the police said, she had no one."

"I would say that's pretty accurate. She was constantly a runaway. No home kept her for very long because she was always slipping out somehow. I worried about her every time I saw her. She just seemed so lost."

"I wish I could have known her."

"I always thought of you when I would see Sera. She looked so much like you as a kid. It was uncanny, really."

We both look down, unsure of what to say that would do justice to the tragedy that is the short life of Seraphina. There really isn't anything you can say to that, is there?

* * *

Hollow Ground. It is the only place in town with decent food and wifi, the obvious choice for an out of town guest trying to get a little work done in this black hole of no cell service. Colby has been spending his days here trying not to miss too much while he's away from the office. I decided to surprise him with a visit, maybe just check up on him to see what he's up to... if he indeed didn't just leave me in the middle of the night. We shall see.

Entering the little coffee shop, he is nowhere in sight and with only five tables I don't think I could miss him. I find myself a seat at the counter and recognize the woman serving up coffee immediately. Della Woods. She lived across the street from Cash when we were growing up. Crankiest women to ever walk the planet. My sincerest hope is that she doesn't recognize me.

"What can I get you?" she asks in her default unhappy tone.

I cringe a little but do my best to hide it as she engages with me, "Um... I was just wondering if my fiancé had been here. He was supposed to meet me here and I'm afraid I missed him."

"How the hell should I know that?" she says with an eye roll. I frown as I pull out my phone and scroll to a picture of Colby. She stares at the screen and shrugs her shoulders. "Never seen him."

That can't be right... "Are you sure? He's been coming here to work for the last couple of days. He said he's been here all day."

"Not my job to keep track of your man for you, but no. I haven't seen him and I'm the only one that keeps this place up and running. I would have seen him if he came in."

My shoulders slump and I drop my face. Not what I was wanting to hear. "Thanks." I start to stand to leave but decide to take advantage of this opportunity while I have it. "Hey, I'm back in town after being gone for a long while and am wanting to reconnect with some old friends. You don't happen to know Cash Perez, do you?"

"Oh, hell. Yeah, I know that whole lousy Perez bunch. Pieces of garbage if you ask me."

Her words sting a little to hear her lump Cash in with the rest of his family, "I know the rest of the family is pretty shady, but Cash was always different when we were growing up. He's a cop in town now, right?"

"He's a cop alright, probably the lousiest one on the force. You don't come from a family like that and not be just like them. He's got a darkness in his eyes that says he's just like the lot of them. You look deep into who that guy is and I bet you find some pretty nasty shit." She winks at me as she walks off into the kitchen with these words and leaves me to ruminate on all her wisdom. I sneak out the front door before she can come back.

What a joyous visit that was... I have always known what Cash's family was like. There was a reason we always hung out at my house. Even with his issues, Dad was always respectful and made efforts to be nice when we had friends over. Cash's dad would knock his mom out right in front of you like it was no big deal. He knocked Cash around too until he grew strong enough to fight back. His mom was no pleasure either. She was loud and mouthy and known to slap her kid around just as much. They were both in and out of jail so many times over the years. It's a wonder they never lost custody of Cash at some point. He would have been better off if they had.

But I've always viewed Cash as the exception to his family. He was never like them. His grandma kept him a lot and she seemed to be where he got the biggest number of his traits. She was so kind and loving. That's how I picture him, like Nana Maya. Then again, what do I know?

Clearly not where my own fiancé is. I know he told me he's been at Hollow Grounds when he's not been at the house with me. Why would he lie? My heart rate speeds up immeasurably as I think about the only obvious answer to that question. One only lies about where he is if he is doing something he shouldn't be.

* * *

I spend the rest of the afternoon with Gabby trying to push aside everything in my head. We talk about every detail of her life for the last ten years. She tells me about her adorable nieces and nephews. We laugh uncontrollably at the idea that her goofy little brother is somehow now a husband and father. She tells me about her job and how much she loves what she does. She tells me what an unbelievable man my brother has grown into and how his students look up to him. I could not be more proud of the two souls Shane and Gabby have become. Discussing their lives has proved to be the perfect distraction and I genuinely have a sense of ease and peace within me by the time Shane comes home from school and joins us.

By the time our take out dinner arrives, I have pretty much decided that Colby isn't coming back. I would deserve that, but it would only put more questions in my mind about who he is. I was sure I knew the answer to that already, deep down I think I still do, yet I can't help but let my current paranoid fear cloud my vision of him.

Just as I have all but given up he walks through the door. There is awkwardness as Shane grumbles, rolls his eyes, and leaves the room. Gabby gives me a weak smile and a reassuring squeeze on my shoulder as she follows him out of the room. Colby comes to sit on the couch with me.

"Hi," he says as he reaches out for my hand.

"Hi." I keep up my best poker face but hesitate to give him my hand.

He looks down at my clear reluctance and frowns, "We've got a lot to talk about, don't we?"

This catches me off guard, but I nod my head in agreement,

94

"What's up?"

"I haven't actually been going to the coffee house to work," he admits.

His confession strikes me like a slap. I didn't even have to ask. I decide to play dumb, "What do you mean? Why?"

"I told you I was working because I didn't want to admit that I was visiting my mom. She's not really all there anymore from all the drugs over the years, but she's still my mom. I just thought that since you were mending things with your brother, maybe I should do the same with her."

I feel like a piece of shit. I've been sitting here all afternoon thinking the absolute worst when I should have known better, "Colby, I think that is great. I'm really happy for you." He smiles at me and I can see that he looks a little lighter than he did a couple of days ago. I don't deserve this man. "I wanted to admit something too if that's okay." He nods before I go on, "I haven't been fair to you for a really long time. Maybe ever. I don't mean to make you feel like you don't matter."

We let this sit between us for a long moment before Colby responds, "Spending time with Mom has really been a wake-up call for me. I was so mad at her for a long time. I held so much against her for how much it sucked to grow up in that house. She apologized to me today and I realized that I could only accept her words because I gave myself the time and distance from it all to process it." He takes my hands now, "I owe you some space and time to process coming home too. I can't expect you to just be okay. I can't magically make you do what I want when you're in the middle of this hugely scary thing for you. Especially with the extra stress right now."

I feel in complete shock. I never expected him to take on the responsibility for how I've acted towards him. I totally don't

95

deserve him, "Colby, none of this is your fault."

He stops me with a raised hand, "I have to let you work through all this. Maybe in the end you decide I'm it, maybe you don't. I'll deal with that when it comes, but I'll be here waiting if you decide you need me."

My heart balloons for this man and I hold his face between my hands, "You really are good as gold, aren't you?"

He laughs sadly, "You give me too much credit."

"It's all deserved."

He smiles and squeezes my hand in answer before getting serious again, "I don't want this to be goodbye."

"It absolutely doesn't have to be."

"Can I stay here until I figure out my next move tomorrow? I think maybe I'll stay with mom for a while. I buried myself in work for so long and I think I just realized maybe that isn't the most important thing."

"Colby, I never intended this to be me kicking you out. You know you're welcome." Just don't tell Shane I said that. With a nod of his head, we sort of put the subject to rest. My head is spinning with what just happened. Just like that, I don't think I'm engaged anymore and I'm not quite sure what to do with that. Suddenly that feels scary and uncertain too. I ask, "You know I still love you, right?"

"Of course. I'm counting on that to get us through this," he says.

\* \* \*

Colby and I went to bed together after our talk. We said nothing, just laid together for the last time maybe ever and held each other's hand. Tonight, his presence in my bed was what I needed to further lay my earlier suspicions of him to rest. He was here to be my friend and support. No ulterior motives are needed when you no longer have a stake in the game.

Now, hours later, the last shreds of what felt like a warm and comforting dream, a miracle considering the week I've had, fade away into nonsense just outside of my grasp as I stir in my warm bed. The room is bright, but the world outside is still black. I turn to the clock on my nightstand to see it is well before daylight will come, yet my bedroom light is shining bright and there seems to be activity outside of the warm cocoon of quilts I am wrapped in.

I sit up to see Colby pacing back and forth across the room in a frenzy. Wiping sleep from my eyes I ask, "What are you doing? It's the middle of the night."

"I thought I could stay here. I thought I could make this work somehow, but I have to go. I can't be here another second," he rambles out.

I'm so confused. "I don't understand. I thought we were okay for now. Just on pause and all that." He turns to face me and he looks crazed. His eyes are wild and I've never seen him like this. "Are you okay?"

"No. I'm not fucking okay," he bellows at me. "You were talking in your sleep. You were saying his name! I can't take it Savannah," he lurches toward the bed and slams his fists on it. "All I have ever wanted was for you to love me like I love you. I've always known you didn't, but it has never hurt as bad as when I hear you say his name in a way that you will never say mine."

"Colby, I was asleep! I'm sorry-" He cuts me off with a raised hand.

"Don't say you're sorry. You're not really sorry." His face is pained and it seems like he can't continue, but he does through gritted teeth, "It's like you've forgotten how much he hurt you! He hurt you so much that you had to leave your own home for a decade and you're still not over it! Yet, still, you can't see him for what he is."

"I was asleep! I have no control over what I do in my sleep!" This is insanity.

He grinds his teeth together and the sound makes me wince, "If he's in your dreams it's because he's in your head!"

"I don't know what you want me to say. Again, I was asleep!"

Colby rolls his eyes, "I want you to say you realize he is who he always has been, that he's never been a good guy! He's a manipulator! He knows exactly what to say and do to get you right in his pocket. He's even got your brother under his spell now. Shane used to see him for what he is, but now he's joined the cult." I sit silent because he's right. My brother hated Cash the entirety of our relationship. He wanted me to have nothing to do with him. Colby can see me turning this over in my head and pounces on my moment of doubt, "Think back to all the things Shane used to say about him. I bet it sounded pretty similar to this, didn't it?" My silence is the only answer he needs and the irrational fury seems to morph into compassionate worry, "I have to go now because it's tearing me apart to watch you fall for him again and you won't let me protect you anyway. You have to figure this out on your own and I trust Shane to keep you safe. He hates me, but he loves you," he puts his hands on my shoulders and looks me in the eye, "Just be careful. He's dangerous and I think if you stop letting him blind you, you'll see it too. All the pieces point to him, Savannah. Make the effort to see it."

The impact of his words hits me like a ton of bricks. Am I just choosing to only see what I want to? Probably... as I ponder this I glance down at the beautiful ring he put on my finger, "For the record, I am sorry for any pain I've caused you. I never meant to hurt you," I say as I place the ring in his hand.

He purses his lips and then places the ring on top of my dresser, "Keep it. I gave it to you. Maybe someday you may even want to wear it again when all this is said and done. Maybe you'll decide to come back to the home we made together. I'll be there waiting if you do." I try to embrace him, but he shrugs me off, "I can't, Savannah. Don't make this harder than it is." He places a soft kiss on my hair and pleads with me one last time, "Look deeper at him. He's not who you think he is."

I let him go in peace and watch silently as he quite literally walks out of my life. I wouldn't call what I'm feeling pain, just more regret. That alone tells me everything I needed to know about our relationship. I should never have dragged him into all this mess. Giving myself over to him had been a choice I made for all the wrong reasons from the very beginning. It was selfish and not at all who I want to be.

# 20

## Savannah

**N**ew beginnings. A new chapter. A total redo.

Those are my goals for this day and every day going forward. Something in me feels renewed and refreshed today and I want to make the most of it. I meet Gabby in the kitchen this morning with a giant cup of coffee ready in hand to see if I can butter her up.

"Gabby, you look beautiful this morning," I gush as she walks into the room.

She fingers her sleep tousled messy bun and gives me serious side-eye, "What do you want?"

"Have some coffee."

"What do you want?" she repeats with narrowed eyes staring me down.

"I was just wondering..." I hesitate. How does someone ask for an almost certainly illegal favor? "I know you said you knew Seraphina from the hospital and I was wondering if you maybe knew where I could get some more information about her."

She stares blankly at me for the longest moment and I begin to think she's going to pretend she didn't even hear me at all,

"Savvy, she was a minor and HIPPA says I shouldn't have even told you she was a patient. I got nothing for you." My hopes plummet and I'm pretty sure I'm making a pouty face. "Stop it with that face, loser," she says with a laugh, "I might have an idea actually."

I immediately perk up, "Really?"

"My little sister, Suzie, is working for the newspaper and I bet you anything she has all kinds of dirt dug up for a story about Sera. Let me call her and see what I can find out for you."

I throw my arms around her and squeeze her so tight, "Thank you, thank you, thank you!"

She excuses herself with her cell already to her ear and I chew my nails while I wait. I can't believe Suzie is old enough to be working anywhere. She was just 12 when I left and thinking of her as an adult with a grown-up job makes me feel about a thousand years old. The idea that she is a reporter for a newspaper is so perfect though. She was always flitting around spreading all the gossip. She didn't even care who it was about, she just wanted to spread the dirt. This makes me giggle.

I have successfully chewed off all ten fingernails by the time Gabby comes back in the room a few minutes later.

"Okay, I've got the scoop. I wrote it all down for you because I have to get ready for work, but Suz said you could feel free to call her if you have any more questions. I wrote her number down for you too, but beware she will probably grill you like crazy if you call," she says with a shrug of the shoulders because that's just who Suzie is. With a kiss on the cheek, Gabby is gone and I am left with not as much information as I had hoped, but at least more than I had before.

*She was abandoned on the sidewalk a couple blocks from the hospital just a few hours old. Wrapped in a blanket that was stitched with the name Seraphina. Born on May 7th, 2006. Severely malnourished and spent 6 months in the hospital for various reasons. Health problems her whole life related to birth defects, never kept long in foster care because of intense medical needs early on.*

Other than the fact that she was born the year following my mom's disappearance, I don't know that I can decipher any real clues from this, but it's a start. I would love to call Suzie and talk more, maybe she forgot something important... but I don't think I can take being grilled for information right now. I do have an idea of one other person I might be able to get a little more info from though...

\* \* \*

Cash doesn't seem quite as surprised to see me when I walk into the police station this time. He gives me a friendly wave and a smile as he comes over to the front desk where I'm waiting for him.

"Can I help you miss?" he asks coyly.

"Would you be able to sit and talk with me for a few minutes?" I ask in answer.

"Yeah, of course. Everything okay?"

I let out a squawking laugh at this, "Okay is a pretty relative term at this point, don't you think?"

He gives me a weak smile and leads me out the front door to a bench, "What's going on, Vannah?"

It is sunny and warm outside today and the sun shining on his face makes him look 20 again. I smile to see him just how I remember him. He smiles back and my stomach does a little flip. I wonder if that will stop if I find out it's him. "I just wanted to talk to you about Seraphina and see if there is anything new you can tell me about the case. I just need to try and put the pieces together in my head because I'm scared and I feel like I'm just kind of out here blowing in the wind."

He lets a harsh breath out as he speaks, "Vannah, I will do everything in my power to keep you safe. That will not ever change, but it's an open investigation and I can't tell you any more than you already know. Even if I could, there's no news. Stuff like this takes a lot longer in real life than on tv. I'm sorry."

I lay it all on the line, "If I am in danger, so are Shane and Gabby. I can't stand having them at risk like this and I know they mean something to you too."

"They do. Very much," he says as he chews his lip. Staring gravely at me, he seems to be making a decision. Lowering his voice he continues, "Listen, the only thing I can tell you can't go past us." I nod. "I mean it, Vannah. You can't even tell Shane because this could be a big break in more than just this case and you're going to want to tell him."

I lock eyes with him, "I promise."

"She had two tattoos," he says, like that alone is some blockbuster reveal.

I frown, "She was a teenage runaway. I'm surprised she didn't have twelve."

He looks around us and leans closer before he continues, "The tattoo looked really old and was all blown out, barely even decipherable. Considering she was only 13, we looked into it. Apparently, she had it already when she was found as a baby."

"Someone tattooed an infant?" I can't believe what I'm hearing.

"Hold on, there's more to it than that. Like I said it was barely more than a blur because it was so old and badly done, but I

103

recognized it immediately and we're looking into it because the timing could work out. It was a daisy on her shoulder blade. All white petals except one blue and one pink petal."

"That was my mom's tattoo."

"Yeah, except this girl had a third colored petal on hers. Just like your mom's with a blue petal for Shane, a pink petal for you, and a purple petal, we can only assume, for Seraphina."

"But Mom was already gone when she was born. I looked into it this morning."

"Well, she was missing already, but we don't know what happened to her. Gone doesn't mean dead. Don't take this as truth because it's just a theory I'm working on, but if you look at the timing, she could have been 8 or so weeks pregnant when she was taken and no one would have ever known. To top it off, the baby was malnourished when she was abandoned. If some lunatic had Beth stashed somewhere all those months, she likely would not have been getting what she needed to keep a baby healthy during pregnancy."

My body feels cold inside and like a lead weight is sitting on my shoulders, "And that could explain why she looked like me."

"Exactly. And why you're being pulled into it all. This could all be the same guy. Whoever took your Mom could be the one that killed Seraphina. I'm talking to the lead detective about reopening the case to see if we can piece together any more clues that could help us find him and maybe find Beth too."

I'm numb now and my words come out barely more than a whisper, "I took a DNA test. They'll know when it comes back."

"I saw that and I'm working on getting it rushed through. It shouldn't be a problem if I can convince them that this guy could be a serial offender. Vannah, this could be the answer to everything."

There is immense joy in his eyes as he tells me that this could solve my mom's case, but all I can feel is crushing remorse, "If it is the same guy, then it was never my dad. It couldn't be. He's been barely functional for years. He couldn't have killed Seraphina."

This connection clicks for Cash and his shoulders slump, "I know, but at least it will give your whole family answers while he's still here. You can't blame yourself for believing what looked like the truth right in front of you." Oh, but I can. I couldn't see any possibility other than my dad's guilt, but I could step right over clues pointing directly at Cash like they didn't exist.

"Thank you for telling me all this. Thank you for trusting me," I tell him numbly.

"You deserve it more than anyone I can imagine. You and Shane both. I want to give it to you and I will do everything I can to solve this for you both."

My gratitude is immense, but where does one find joy under the weight of all that? I give him the only slight smile I can muster, "I have to go. I'll keep it all to myself for now."

As I stand to leave, he reaches for my hand and my eyes flutter at the all too familiar feeling of his touch. I gaze down at him as he stares at my now naked ring finger and slides a fingertip gently across the tan line from the ring I no longer wear. He seems lost for words for a moment, but then pretends he didn't notice, "Vannah, please be careful. Make sure all the doors and windows are locked and stick close to Shane, okay?"

I nod my head before leaving without a word.

# 21

# Savannah

My original intention after leaving Cash at the police station was to go home. Home, home. St Louis home. I planned to drive straight there and pretend these last few days never happened, to completely erase my presence from every life I have touched here. I don't want to hurt any of them any more than I already have and they would all be better off without me. I clearly know nothing that I thought I did.

Instead, I find myself parked in front of James River Rehabilitation and Long Term Care. I need to see him. I need to look into his face and tell him I'm sorry that I never believed him, that I couldn't look beyond my own narrow world view. I have to do that because every single word Cash shared with me today rang true. It all clicked together and rang a bell in my soul. It is crazy, insane, and nearly impossible to believe it could ever be rooted in reality, but that's what makes it the most plausible explanation for everything. Reality is always stranger than fiction.

I walk into my father's room and find Shane already here.

His eyes are red-rimmed and tired. We seem to be an equally matched pair.

"Why aren't you at school?" I ask.

"Didn't they call you too?" he asks with gravel in his voice.

"Who? No. No one called."

He lowers his head and comes to stand by my side, "The nursing staff called and suggested we start seriously planning for the end. The doctors don't think he has much time left at all now. I came to look through some of his stuff and see if I can find his old journal. He had what he wanted written in it and I just want him to have that, whatever it is." Shane has tears welling in his eyes and I embrace him as tightly as I can. "I know this probably isn't on your to-do list today so you don't have to-"

"I want to help. Where do you think it would be?"

His face is so grateful, "I have no clue. He hasn't been able to write in it since the first month or two he was here. It could be anywhere. Literally anywhere." We both look around the room at the years' worth of just stuff piled on top of dressers and nightstands. This could be a long search, but at least we're searching together.

Shane is boiling over with nervous energy. He has been actively dreading this moment for a very long time. I never even took the time to think about how hard this was going to be on him every time I made a swipe at Dad when we were younger and I wish I could take it all back. I never want my brother to hurt and feel alone in his pain ever again. For that reason, and that reason alone, I will not run again. I will be here and I will dig through everything our father has ever owned to make it all right again. While I take my time, slowly sifting through a closet of junk, Shane is frantically flinging open cabinets and drawers. He has no control over his churning emotions.

As I comb my way through a stack of mostly unused crossword books, I hear a drawer being flung open and then Shane gasps.

"Did you find it?" I call out hopefully.

"Oh fuck. Oh shit. Oh no," Shane yells out from behind me. I spin around to look just as he folds himself in half and dry heaves in the trash can next to our father's bed.

I rush to his side, "Shane! Are you okay?" He can't even speak. He simply points to the last drawer he opened as he heaves over the trash can once more.

Slowly I make my way across the room and peer down into the drawer. For a moment my brain can't make sense of what I'm seeing. Why would there be a beautifully manicured mannequin's hand in this drawer? But then I noticed the red pooling beneath it. I see the imperfection of hangnails and sloppy fingernails painted in a hurry. I see the indentation made on its finger beneath the beautiful diamond ring it's wearing. Finally, it all clicks together in my head. That's a hand. A real woman's severed hand is resting quietly in the drawer of my father's bedside table. I can't move. I can't look away. My heartbeat is pounding so loudly in my ears that it is all I can hear but I can't look away. I'm sure I must be wrong. I reach down to touch it and find it cold and dry, but unmistakably human. I don't even realize I'm screaming until outside noise bursts into the room. I hear him before I see him.

"Vannah, what's happening?! What's wrong?!" Cash has really impeccable timing, doesn't he? Why is he even here? "Vannah?! Vannah, what is it?!"

Like Shane before me, I simply point into the drawer as I stumble my way backward, trying to distance myself from it. Cash peers inside and I go to embrace my brother who is just beginning to recover from his nausea. Cash quickly looks away from the severed hand and has gone ghost white. His face looks like he may be sick as well. Not missing a beat, he goes into cop mode and begins delegating orders. He tells the nursing staff to lock down the facility, no one in and no one out. He tells the friendly orderly I met my first day here to call 911 and report what's happened. He then comes over to us and whispers to Shane a long string of instructions before turning to me.

"Vannah, Shane is going to take you somewhere safe. He knows where to go. I-"

"Wait, why do I have to go? You said no one leaves and I'm a witness. I want to know what's happening!"

"Listen," he pleads as he holds my face in his hands, "I will explain everything when we get this scene secured and I can get out of here, but, please, for now just go with Shane. Please."

His eyes are pleading and scared. I know I need to listen just looking at his eyes, "Okay."

Just like that, I'm being ushered out of the room by my brother and this whole thing feels like a feverish dream. I steal a last look at Cash and he is staring at the contents of the drawer. He, like me, is mesmerized somehow and can't look away, but the emotions in his gaze are different than mine had been. Where I had been shocked and devastated, he seems afraid in a way I don't understand. He is frightened on a level beyond what anyone would expect and I am left with nothing but wondering.

# 22

# Savannah

Shane and I ride together in silence. We've got nothing left after this week. We drive and drive, way past our house and farther out into the trees. We finally pull up in front of a sprawling log cabin and Gabby rushes out to meet us. Shane rushes to her and she embraces him, both looking emotional beyond measure. Gabby welcomes us both into her home and the lovers disappear into her bedroom to give them the privacy they need to support each other through the emotional roller coaster that seems to just be our life now.

I sit solemnly on the couch and try to process it all on my own. I don't have a someone to share my burden with anymore and I feel so cold and alone, far more than I ever thought I could. Hours pass and I do nothing but stare into the empty space before me. I seem to be doing a lot of that lately. Gabby comes out a few times to check on me, but I assure her I'm okay.

"Sure you are," she finally tells me around 11:30pm as she comes to sit with me on the couch I've been restlessly cocooned on all night.

"How's Shane holding up?" I ask, laying my head over on her

shoulder.

"He'll be okay," she says, "He acts like the tough guy, but he's really a big softie." We both share a soft laugh, "He will be okay though."

"Thank you for being there for him," I tell her with sincere depth in my voice.

She doesn't say anything for a long time and seems to be lost in some deep thought. Finally, she says, "Can I ask you a personal question? I don't want to be nosey or sound rude." I lean back to look at her. I nod as she continues, "I mean this with so much love, I promise, but what happened to the Savannah that could make anything happen if she wanted it enough? You were unstoppable."

The question stings a little and I'm not even sure what to say. I want to be offended, but I'm sure that's just pride talking. Instead, I stutter out, "I... I... I guess... life just happened. Kind of sucked the fight out of me."

She thinks about this for a moment, "No, I think it's more than that. Life happened to all of us, but you seem like someone put out all the fire you had in you. It's like someone told you that you couldn't be your own hero anymore."

I let her words settle over me and really sink in. At first, I want to be angry because it feels like she's calling me weak, but then I push all that anger away because I don't want her to be mad at me. That is the precise moment I realize how right she is. She lets me sit with my realization until I'm able to gather words in response, "I don't know how to fix that."

My words tumble out in a choked-up mess and Gabby gives me a squeeze, "Just reclaim your power, Savvy. Don't let someone tell you that you have to be the victim. Don't let life just happen to you. Fight for it like you used to."

At what moment did I stop doing that?

We sit quietly together for a while and just let it all marinate. I'm grateful for her continued friendship and her ability to tell me like it is. I know she is looking out for me and I can't thank her enough for giving me this shoulder to lean on while I remember how to stand alone.

Eventually, we hear the crunch of gravel outside and look up to see a police cruiser in the driveway. Cash. My heartbeat speeds up just knowing he's here.

"Want me to stay with you?" Gabby asks.

"No, I'm good. I want a minute with him."

She eyes me skeptically, "Behave yourself, young lady."

"Yes, ma'am," I say with a mock salute.

Gabby climbs up from the couch and begins to make her way back to the bedroom but stops short, "Listen, I love Shane, really and truly, but I don't need him to complete me. He's a wonderful man and beautiful addition to my life, but I can stand on my own. That man in the car out there is a phenomenal human being and would genuinely do anything in the world that you ever wanted, but you don't need him to save you. You are plenty capable of saving yourself." My heart warms at her words. I thank her with a smile. She seems hesitant to leave me but relents when I insist.

Cash sits behind the wheel for a long time doing his own staring into nothingness. The wait is maddening. Finally, I see him climb out and I rush to meet him at the door. I fling the door open wide before he even has a chance to knock. I want to immediately start flinging questions at him, but he just looks so tired.

"Hi, Vannah."

I use a weak smile to welcome him inside. He rakes his hands down his face and comes through the door. Turning to face me now, "Can I just hug you for a second?"

I feel an unexpected thrill at his words, "Of course."

He seems surprised that I said yes and locks eyes with me as he hesitates for a moment. Then, with a hard swallow, he slowly closes the distance between us, never looking away from my eyes. As he comes to stand so close that our bodies are touching, I think he might actually kiss me and my breath catches at the thought, but he doesn't. Instead, he wraps his arms around me and pulls me tight against him. My head still fits perfectly into the hollow of his neck and he smells like the cologne I used to buy him every Christmas. The heat of him makes me feel like I might melt right into him. Our breathing has slowed and our bodies have lost the rigid tightness of the day's tension. This is the most comfort I have felt in so many years.

After what feels like the most glorious eternity and still not nearly long enough, he pulls away. For just a second, I refuse to let him. He laughs quietly, barely audible, and ends the embrace. I feel cold as soon as his touch is gone.

Taking my hand, he leads me to the couch, "I've officially been removed from the case."

"What? Why?" This was the last thing I expected him to tell me.

"The hand. It is connected to me. Well, to both of us in a roundabout way."

"How is that even possible?" I ask, incredulous.

Cash sighs, "There was a ring on the hand, a really unique ring engraved with a message."

I don't understand, "How does that connect it to us?"

"I had that ring made for you before you left. Our names are engraved inside the band."

The floor falls out from beneath me. I know my face has lost all its color. My ring; the ring I never knew existed, the ring I ran away from without even knowing. "How did it end up... where it did?"

"No clue. I've had it hidden away in my dresser for all these years. I never even realized anyone else knew it still existed. They are at my house now checking for signs of forced entry or any clues to how someone got their hands on it. They're also checking into the hand and where it came from. It seems it was removed from a live victim so we are searching for her."

I think I might be sick, "She's alive? They cut her hand off while she was still alive?"

He nods his head sadly, "Pretty sick, but at least that means we still may be able to save her."

Silence falls between us and I know we are both thinking about my mom. Had there been a period of time when we could have saved her too? Had she been kept alive having who knows what done to her? It's horrifying to think about and Cash squeezes my hand in a gesture of support. He had been my pillar of strength through that time. He was there every step of the way. No matter where our relationship stands now, I have no doubt we will always share the bond of that experience. Mom had meant so much to him as well and we both lost her that day.

He wipes away the silent tear on my cheek and stands to leave the room without another word. Just as he is about to walk out the door he turns to face me again, "I would have loved you forever, Vannah."

As soon as the words have left his lips, he is out the door and gone.

I give myself a moment to absorb all that just happened before calling out behind me, "You can stop lurking now."

Shane peeks around the corner and waves, "I didn't want to interrupt."

"You were probably hoping we'd make out," I try to joke.

"Eww. You're my sister," he says with a soft smile. We both needed a moment of light-heartedness, but it didn't seem to lighten the mood like we hoped it would.

"Did you hear all the details?" I ask.

"For the most part. Pretty fucked up."

I nod and think to myself for a minute or two, "Hey, can I ask you something?"

He comes to sit with me on the couch, "Well, yeah."

"How did you become friends with Cash?"

"Funny story. We beat the shit out of each other and then we were fine," he chuckles a little, "He's a good dude."

"I'm just going to ignore that caveman answer and try again. How do you go from hating someone to hanging out and having a beer together every night?"

He gives me a slight smile, "We bonded through our total confusion over you."

"Hilarious."

"It's true though. Plus, he's never stopped trying to find out what happened to mom."

My heart feels warm hearing this, if Shane only knew, "What do you mean?"

"That's why he goes to see dad every morning. That's why he was there today. He's hoping some clue might slip out of him in his sleep or something. He still checks in with other possible witnesses too. I know he loved mom, and she loved him too, like one of her own, but I also think he has been convinced that solving her case would bring you back home."

I bow my head and feel guilty for ever thinking any different about Cash, "That's really sweet."

He nods solemnly, "Yeah, it is. So why the curiosity?"

"Promise not to judge me?"

"I mean, I'll definitely judge you, but I'll still love you anyway."

I roll my eyes and continue sheepishly, "Trying to wrap my head around what I really think is going on. Everything is tied to Cash as much as it's tied to me."

"Oh, fuck that mother fucker. I know Colby wants you to think it is all Cash, but he has no clue what he's talking about. He's talking out his ass to try and keep you. The little chicken shit."

"Colby left last night. We're not together anymore, but he wasn't a bad guy," I say quietly.

Shane raises an eyebrow, "Seems to me, he is the one that has you fooled."

"He's never been anything more than a complete gentleman with me. Seriously, he is the nicest guy ever. Nicer than I deserve."

"And that alone doesn't worry you?" he asks. "No one is perfect. We all have flaws and anyone who pretends not to is hiding something serious. He's too nice, Savvy, in a creep kind of way. I bet in everyday life, he never seems to do anything wrong. He controls his emotions so much all the time that sometimes he just snaps, doesn't he?" I nod my head, "And then he bottles it all back down again, just like that. Like flipping a switch."

"That's just his personality. You don't know him. You've spent maybe five minutes with him."

"But I knew him back then and he was a creep then too. I used to catch him just watching you sometimes. I can't tell you how many times I had to threaten him to leave you alone. The fact that he just showed back up in your life by chance hundreds of miles from home? No way that was a coincidence."

I swallow hard letting that all hit me, but still trying to defend, "I doubt he was actually watching me, we just had the same social circles. We were always in the same places."

"No, it was more than that. It was fucking weird and it made me feel super uncomfortable as your brother."

"He was Cash's friend. He was my friend. One of us would have noticed something." I'm grasping for straws now.

"Did you know Gabby is a nurse in the emergency room?" I nod my head, "She was there the night Colby got hurt. The nurses all think he did all that to himself."

I think back to that night and the gravity of what I thought happened next to the reality of how simple it all really was, but no. There is no way someone would bash in their own head. It was insanity to believe that and I tell Shane just that, "No. No way. I can't believe that. This isn't a soap opera."

"Just listen, the cops agreed. They couldn't find any reason to investigate because the injuries appeared self-inflicted. When someone asked him if maybe he was just confused, maybe he fell or something, he lost his fucking shit, Savvy. He exploded in a rage, but not for long. Within a minute he got it all back under control and pretended like nothing had ever happened. Gabby saw it and it really scared her. She said it was like some crazy Jekyll and Hyde shit."

This detail of Colby's personality isn't a surprise to me. He has always had a strange ability to control his reactions to what he's feeling. His anger is fiery and intense, but always quickly managed. I've always admired that about him, his unending supply of self-control, and I've never, not even once, felt unsafe in his presence, "I just can't see him being dangerous. He's not that type of guy. He's.... almost submissive, definitely not domineering. He just has a temper, we all do, and he works really hard to keep it under control. I think that's admirable."

Shane rolls his eyes at this, "Or it's just a sneak peek at who he is under the surface."

I shake my head, "I all but told him I was staying here for Cash. He willingly left. I didn't have to force him. I didn't even have to ask him. He realized on his own that what we were doing wasn't working and he bowed out. I'm giving him the credit he deserves for that because he made my life so much easier than he had to. I didn't deserve that break. I was the asshole in our situation and he didn't have to be understanding. Not to mention, he doesn't live here anymore either. He hasn't been around to be murdering teenagers. I don't think he is anything but a good guy, maybe much more complicated than I took the time to notice, but a good guy. Besides, he left to see his mom yesterday. He's not even here anymore."

Shane seems less than convinced, but he lets the subject go for now, "Cash is genuinely a good guy. You knew that then, even when I didn't. Don't let someone who doesn't know him talk you out of that. I only hated him then because the only thing I knew about him was that he was trying to bang my baby sister."

Keeping a completely straight face, I cut in, "Oh, he was doing more than trying."

"You're disgusting and I'm moving on," he says with an exacerbated sigh. "If I had known then what I know now, I would have given him a chance." He gives me a weak smile and starts back toward the bedroom, "And for the record, my distaste for Colby has nothing to do with thinking he might steal you away because I don't think you are interested in being with him. I could tell the moment I saw you with him. What you want might not still be Cash, but it definitely isn't Colby." With a shrug of his shoulders, he disappears into his bedroom and leaves me alone with my thoughts.

# 23

# Savannah

I'm starting to think sleep and I simply are not friends anymore. I just got out of bed and I'm already exhausted. I rake my hands down my face as I stare out the beautiful picture window in the kitchen. Gabby has a spectacular home, but all I see in the trees surrounding it are secrets.

"Contemplating life?" asks a voice from behind me. I jump and spill the coffee on the counter in front of me. I had expected to be alone after Shane and Gabby both checked on me before leaving for work so turning to see Cash walking into the kitchen behind me is alarming, to say the least, "You about gave me a heart attack! What are you doing here?"

He chuckles to himself as he reaches for the coffee pot, "Well, my house was a crime scene last night so here I am. I snuck back in about 3:00 AM." He leaves his steaming mug on the counter and walks over to me with a dishtowel. He brushes against me as he mops up my coffee mess. Meeting my eyes and making the butterflies in my stomach take flight, "How are you doing this morning?"

I slide my body away from his as I respond, "Okay, considering."

"You don't have to lie."

I let out a deep gust of breath I didn't even realize I had been holding, "I'm pretty much a mess. Thanks for asking."

"Not doing much better myself," he says with a sad smile. Throwing the coffee-soaked towel into the sink, Cash comes to lean against the counter beside me, letting his body just barely touch mine. We don't say anything for a long time. We just share the space, but the quiet is never, for a second, awkward. Finally breaking the silence, he says, "Putting all this chaos to the side, if you can, how have you really been? Since you've been gone. What did you do with the last ten years of your life?" I want to say, try to forget you, but that seems mildly obsessive and not a good response to go with. Other than that I'm at a loss. How do I answer that?

"I... uh... well, I really love my job," is the only thing that feels worth sharing.

"Hmm... let me guess. Something with kids or books."

I can't help but smile up at him, "Both, actually. I'm the youth services coordinator for the public library system."

He smiles back, "That's perfectly you. I'm willing to bet you are amazing at it." I beam with pride. I am good at my job, really good, and it feels amazing to be reminded. Before I came home, we only ever talked about Colby's work. "I can tell you love it," he says, "Your eyes light up even just thinking about it."

"I do. I work really hard because I love being there." We share another comfortable silence before I go on, "What about you? What did you do with ten whole years?"

He smiles that secret smile we used to share just between us, "Well, believe it or not, I'm not actually a cop."

"What?" I ask, not sure where this leads but certain there must be a punch line.

"I'm actually a stripper dressed as a cop and everyone just assumes. Gave me my own big desk and everything." I laugh out loud and shove him with my shoulder. He laughs too but says, "I'm a little offended that you find that so funny."

I roll my eyes, "Oh, please. We both know you wouldn't have any trouble selling tickets to your strip show."

Cash mock dusts his shoulder off, "What can I say? The ladies love me."

That line hits me pretty hard in the gut because I know it's true. The ladies have always absolutely loved him. I know I have zero right to be jealous, seriously ZERO RIGHT, but that doesn't stop me from feeling it anyway. Almost under my breath and while actively avoiding all eye contact, I inquire, "Any one of those ladies in particular that you found to be quite special to you?" I sound like an idiot.

I can feel him staring down at me, "Why Miss Vannah Raymore, why ever do you ask?"

I know he's teasing me and I can feel the mortified heat slowly climbing up my neck and into my cheeks in giant red splotches. I glare up at him, "I had no right to ask that. Just curious. Don't worry about it," before immediately averting my gaze once more.

He moves his body to stand directly in front of me and lifts my chin so I must look directly into his face, "There have been women, I'm not a monk, but there has never been a you."

I suck in a deep breath and feel the immediate change in the atmosphere. It suddenly feels almost humid in the middle of November. His body presses closer to mine. I bite my lip, he licks his. I am certain you can hear my heart beating outside of my body. He lifts me off the floor and places me on the counter in front of him as he comes to stand between my thighs. His eyes move to take in every inch of my face, looking for the past or permission. I'm not sure which. I want to beg him for more; for his lips on mine, his lips everywhere. I want to cry out for him. I want to scream his name, my lips missed saying his name, but I am silent. We just stare at each other, unsure if this is really what the other wants or if old familiar patterns are just easy to fall back into.

"I don't know if this is a good idea," he says softly.

"It's probably most definitely not," I respond breathlessly.

"We should absolutely not do this," he says, still moving dangerously closer.

"Really not smart to do," I say without breaking our intense eye contact.

"To hell with being smart," he says as his hands grip my waist, pressing our bodies together.

"It's really overrated," I say as I tilt my head back, waiting for our mouths to collide.

And then his phone rings.

The loud clatter of a cellphone on the marble countertop scares us both and Cash jumps back away from me like he's been burned. He rushes to silence it and drags his hands down his face. He looks like he is full of regret and I feel like I want to vomit.

"That's work," he says. "And reality," he adds with a dry laugh. "I've got to get going. See you later, okay?"

I nod my head and watch him retreat out of the room. I'm such an idiot. Why in the world would I think a decade passing between us would ever allow us to be what we were?

\* \* \*

After I put myself as back together as possible and slapped my own wrist for letting myself get so worked up this morning, I needed to get out of the house. I am breaking everyone's rules as they all strictly told me not to leave the secluded house in the woods with a security system, but what they don't know and all that... so I decided to finish the journey I started last night. I hopped in an Uber and now here I am.

It's different this time. It feels different to be here. It's still cold and lonely. It still feels sterile and unwelcoming, but something inside me is different this time. I am looking at my father in the bed before me and I no longer hate him. I regret the years I lost with him and how terribly I treated him. I put the blame on him when he had nothing to do with it. I will likely never forgive myself for that. At least I still have time to tell him I'm sorry. I can still hold his hand and whisper to his ears, but I have no way of knowing if he can hear me.

Still, though, the change of heart gives this place new life for me. I notice, this time, the sounds of old men and women laughing as they play bridge, the pitter-patter of little feet as they rush to meet grandparents. I can see the red blush of life in my father's cheeks. I am so thankful for that. I feel that, even though I robbed him of so much more, at least I can give him this time.

I squeeze his hand and lay my cheek against his skin. How did I ever let so many years go by? I think back to every time I began to wonder if it had all been a mistake. I think about all the times I almost came home, that I grew up enough to wonder if there was an option other than my dad. I spent so many days in those first 5 years wondering if I had done the right thing. I was right on the verge of coming back, I even had my apartment packed up and ready to go, when Colby came back into my life. The perfect circumstances would have had to fall into the perfect place for that night to happen the way it did, but I was so scared then that I didn't think too deeply into it. A tall masked man broke into my apartment, held a knife to my throat, penned me down on my bed, and began tearing at my clothes. He got scared and ran away right before my new neighbor, who just happened to be Colby, burst in to save me.

He saved my life that night, at least I've always thought he did. Now, that I sit here in the presence of a man I demonized unfairly for so long, I can remember with perfect clarity all the times Colby talked me in circles until I decided to hate my father again. I was so vulnerable and weak then. He played on my fear and insecurity. I would have believed anything he told me. He wanted me to stay there with him and he manipulated me into doing it by making me feel like I was helpless without him, that I could never make it on my own. Little by little, away from his influence, things are coming into focus for me and I am feeling a lot less guilty about letting him go.

I gaze up at another puzzle in my life now, my father. Seemingly in a deep and peaceful sleep, I wonder if somehow he holds the answers in there somewhere. I refused to speak to him after mom was gone, but what if I had? Could my memories and experiences have met with his to put together the pieces of what happened that night? Could we have saved her together?

I brush my hand across his cheek, feeling the rough stubble of his face, and make a mental note to come back with a shaving kit later. How different would both of our lives be right now if I had just taken the time to see other possibilities? With that thought, I can feel the tears pricking at my eyes, but I refuse to let them fall. I am done crying. I'm done feeling sorry for myself. It's time to move forward instead of staying rooted in past trauma. I've let myself be the victim for far too long. I'm better than that. He raised me to be better than that. He taught me how to fight and stand up for myself. He would be so disappointed in what I let myself become. I will do better for him. Consider that my gift to him for all the times he told me he loved me and I didn't understand.

With that thought, I kiss my father's head and quietly make my way out of the room. I move as if I am afraid I'll wake him. Wishful thinking. As I make my way into the hallway, Cash is leaning against the nurse's station in front of me because, of course he is.

"How are you always here?" I ask with an instant furrowed brow.

"I was here to see your dad and didn't want to interrupt your time with him," he says with a soft smile. "I figure it was long overdue." I nod but say nothing and walk around him. He reaches out for my hand and stops me, "Can I talk to you for just a minute?"

I can't tell him no, "Sure. What's up?"

"I just wanted to clarify about this morning—"

My stomach clenches and I cut him off with frantic shaking of my head, "Nope, we're good. Don't need to have that conversation."

"I just want you to understand—"

"I get it. You were just falling into the old routine and we let our emotions get the best of us. It's fine. No hard feelings," I say, knowing it's a lie. I'm all ready to turn over a new leaf as the strong girl, but I am feeling way too raw and vulnerable to hear him say he doesn't want me right now.

His face is confused and slightly hurt, "Vannah..." He trails off, looking unsure of how to continue. Finally, speaking almost just to himself, "I don't know how he stole your self-worth, but I could kill him for it."

I have no idea how to respond to this. Twice in twenty-four hours has someone in my life eluded to this same thing and I'm not sure yet what to do with it. I simply look back at this man before me and give him a weak shrug of my shoulders.

He pulls me closer and looks down at me, "You have value. You always have and always will." My cheeks flush and I look down at our feet.

I want to believe him and I want to give in and let him hold me while I cry into his shoulder for days, but what good will that do either of us? My hand is still in his and I glance down at the connection. I squeeze his fingers in mine and then let go as I walk alone down the long, cold corridor.

# 24

# Savannah

Back safely inside the walls of Gabby's home, I pace the floors full of nervous energy but securely protected by an elaborate alarm code and the occasional police drive by. I am crawling out of my skin being here alone with nothing but my own thoughts for company. The woman doesn't even own a tv. She has maybe ten books in the whole place and they are all about science and medicine. We are not the same.

I finally find a deck of cards and challenge myself to a serious solitaire marathon, but after fourteen losses in a row, I call it quits. I feel like I've been here staring at my own reflection in the giant windows for six hours, but a quick glance at my phone proves it's only been about two hours. I am pretty sure I'm going to lose my mind here.

Looking down at my phone again, my fingertips begin to feel itchy and I chew on the inside of my bottom lip as I think about calling someone. In my current state, that would be a terrible idea, but what else is there to do? I don't have a fancy phone with games and internet access at my fingertips like a normal human being. Why? Because Colby said we didn't need that kind of distraction in our lives. I feel instantly angry when I make the connection between deleting technology from my life and an ability to isolate me from everyone I used to know.

Furious texting fingers make their way to his name in my inbox and I start to type a really nasty message to him, but then I catch a glimpse of the last text he sent me: *I didn't say that. I think you're imagining things.* That one text on its own seems harmless enough, but it strikes a chord in me. I begin scrolling through everything he has sent me for as long as I've had this phone and I can't believe what I'm seeing. How have I never put this all together before?

*You're upset over nothing.*

*I didn't do that. You're remembering it all wrong.*

*I think maybe you made that up.*

*Remember how bad it went last time? You need my help.*

*You must be confused again.*

*Just calm down. I'll fix it for you.*

*You're not really upset over that, are you?*

*It's okay. I still love you even when you screw up.*

*You're crazy.*

*You're crazy*

*You're crazy.*

*You're crazy.*

With each text I read, I feel more and more enraged. None of these things were said to me jokingly or out of kindness. They were said to put me in a position of need, to make me feel like less than. They were used strategically to invalidate every emotion or thought I was having. To make me feel so crazy that I can't make my own decisions and it worked.

I have been an emotional mess since the moment I stepped foot back in this town and it's no wonder! For the first time in forever, I am actually feeling what comes naturally instead of being told I'm crazy for feeling it! No wonder I question every single thing I say and do! I've had a little voice in my life telling me I can't or I'm not competent enough to do that on my own for five fucking years!

No. Not just five years. All the way back to high school. I remember now. He would say little things here or there. I always thought it was just his way of being nice, but now... my locker would jam and he would confidently tell me the "right way" to close it. I was just doing it wrong. Good thing he was there to do it for me. He always wanted to help me learn to drive because I "could really use the help". I would think Cash had asked me to wait for him after school and Colby would laugh and say I must be crazy... Cash never said that... let me give you a ride instead.

It's just little things, but it all adds up to manipulation and I feel so stupid. I let him get away with that. Shane, Gabby, and Cash were all right. It really was him pulling the strings in my life to his own advantage, to pull me down to his level. Suddenly all the pieces fall together in my head. The second guessing. The uncertainty and fear. All of it was preyed upon and exploited for personal gain. I feel cheated out of all the lost years. I feel angry that it was manipulated out of my grasp. I want to call and rage at him, but what good will that accomplish? He'll probably just call me crazy again.

What, then, can I do? What is the best way to get even with an abuser that stole your potential away? To reclaim what they stole. Stand on my own two feet and take it all back. Take back the life I should have lived. Claim joy and just live to spite them. That's what I need to do.

* * *

I have been running from this man for the last 10 years of my life. The need to do so was pounded into me over and over again until I forgot my own free will. I forgot that I was allowed to choose. I lived those years terrified to venture out of routine because I might fully feel what I did to myself and I was constantly being told I would fail. Now, as I embrace a return to everything I left behind, the thrill of my late night spontaneity has me exhilarated in ways I haven't felt since I was 20.

I laid it all out for Gabby when she finally came home from a long 12-hour shift. I expected her to congratulate me on finally not being an idiot, but she had even better to offer. With a deep hug and giddy squeals she offered her assistance to go "save that lonely man". She drove me over herself. I feel like I am doing something wrong but in the most wonderful ways possible. This must be what it feels like to be a Bond girl on a covert mission.

I used to admire this house when we were kids. It wasn't that different from my own childhood house, but my house lacked the needed upkeep that having an alcoholic dad prevented from happening. I see that Cash has kept it up as well as I remember. It makes me smile as I hit my knuckles against the perfect blue front door, but panic twists my gut as soon as I hear the thudding knock echo through the house. What am I doing? It's after midnight. He is probably going to shoot me because he thinks I'm an intruder or he's just going to think I've lost my mind. I'm an idiot... but then he opens the door and I remember that second guessing is no longer allowed to be a part of my life.

He reflects my own relief as the tension in his body relaxes when he sees it's me, "What are you doing here, Vannah?"

Only the truth will fit this moment, "I just decided this is where I should be."

"What does that mean?" he asks with hopeful skepticism in his golden eyes.

Without a word, I place my hand on his bare chest and feel his heart beating against my palm. He places his own hand over mine and watches the loving delight that crosses my face to be allowing his presence in my life again after all these years. In one fluid motion, he pulls me into his arms and closes the door behind me. For just a moment he stares down at me, asking for my permission, then I meet him in the middle where our lips collide in what must be the most hard-earned kiss of all time. Explosions of sultry heat set me on fire and his soft moan against my lips makes me crave a deeper connection.

Cash presses my body against the door and breaks our kiss to shower my neck with soft kisses and gentle tugging bites. My flesh is on fire for him. I forgot that I could ever feel this good with just a man's touch. This man's touch. He places his cheek against mine and his breathy voice against my ear sends chills through my quaking body.

"Is this really happening?" he asks, short of breath.

I take his face in my hands and force him to see me here with him, "If it's a dream, I don't want to wake up."

He crashes his mouth against mine again and we are all hands. Making out like the two teenagers we were when we first fell in love, we fumble our way to his bedroom, never for a second breaking our connection. We fall to the bed and the rest is history. There will be no coming back from this. There is so much heat between us right in this very moment that every version of our former selves has burned to the ground. We are forever etched into each other's souls as permanently as our

132

matching tattoos. Every move of his greedy hands across my skin. Every kiss I place on his bare chest and neck. Every single piece of clothing torn off and thrown carelessly to the floor. All of it is like coming home after being gone for far too long.

Our heavy breathing matches the rhythm of the aching bedsprings, creating the most seductive melody I have ever heard. Every thrusting move he makes is calculated and designed to make me cry out in bone-deep pleasure. He takes his time doing all the right things, all the things that make me come undone.

He really does still know what I like.

My body trembles beneath him and the crazed hunger in his eyes betrays his equal need for me. Every moment that passes, the exquisite pressure builds inside us both. We claw at each other, desperate for an even deeper embrace until we both explode as a shared climax crashes down on us.

In complete satisfaction, Cash's weight falls on me as I lay still quaking beneath him. Our hurried breaths match one another and the sweaty sheen on our bodies binds us together. I savor every single second of his body on mine. I can still feel him inside of me when he braces himself over me, covering me in a flurry of kisses along my jawline and down my neck. He nuzzles his rough stubble against my skin and with a gentle kiss on my lips, he lays his soul bare saying, "I don't think I can take it if you leave again."

Sucking in my breath, I cradle his face in my hands, "I almost didn't survive it the first time I did." Our lips meet again, tenderly exploring a love that time never forgot. He bites at my lip in that soft, slow way that makes my insides melt. I gently speak against his lips as he continues to drive me wild, "Marry me, Cash."

He looks up and makes eye contact with me, brimming over with emotion, " Vannah, I... I should have years ago."

With my words, I feel him take over my body once again. Over and over, I let him take me places I had forgotten existed until the heat of the morning sun shines on our exhausted bodies.

# 25

# Colby

I t blows my mind how hard it has been to mold her mind into what I wanted it to be all these years. I have said all the same things to her that I have said to everyone else in my life, yet she has always resisted. There has always been... something in her that refused to just be compliant. It is absolutely maddening.

The moment she told me she was coming home, I knew that the game had just been changed. I saw a spark of that firey light in her eyes coming back after I had spent years trying to douse it. I knew I was going to have to up my game, but I didn't realize just how far that would lead me into depravity. No turning back now, though.

I had to paint the one she was running back to as the worst possible kind of human. I had to make her hate him. It was the only way. If not, she'd be right back in his arms and, well, that just wouldn't do.

The tattoo on Sera should have been enough. It wasn't. Turns out, tracking down her juvenile delinquent sister she didn't even know existed was a whole lot easier than it was to ditch her way back in the day. I knew it was her the second I saw her hitchhiking just outside of town. She couldn't look more like my Savannah if she tried, just a little rougher around the edges. I had to squeeze the life out of her with my own hands, the only bright side to the whole debacle. I had to scrap my makeshift tattoo machine back together and somehow remember how to fucking use it after thirteen fucking years. I had to put her body where Savannah might find it. That was a lot of fucking work just to frame a guy, but apparently not enough for my girl!

The bracelet, placed so perfectly so she would be the one to find it, didn't even make a dent in her resolve. I knew she would go to her mother and I knew she would make the connection, but did she run from her precious Cash?! No, she put the fucking thing on her own fucking wrist! I lost it after that. I completely went off the edge. I tried to rally and stay with her while I figured the rest out, but I couldn't do it. I had to be away from it all. I was going to blow it all and I had entirely too much invested at that point. I had to get more aggressive. I really thought the next one would do it.

A mother fucking severed human hand wearing a ring he bought for her! Not even that cracked her faith in that fucking waste of human life!!! If anything, it pushed her closer to him. She disappeared off my radar that night, but the very next night I see her on his front porch! She went to bed with him. She let him touch her. She let him inside her. I wanted to be sick. I wanted to burst through the door and tear him to shreds right then! I should have, but no... I'm better than that. I pulled it all together. I made my final move.

I had the perfect body to create my next scene with and, as I laid it out lovingly in the darkened city park, I made sure Cash Perez was written all fucking over it.

# 26

# Savannah

Waking up in this bed is the greatest feeling of contentment that I can imagine. This is where I am supposed to be. I should have been here all along.

Cash is beaming as he walks into the bedroom with a tray of breakfast. He made me promise to stay here and I giggled as I listened to him cuss and stumble his way through cooking me a stack of slightly charred pancakes and half raw bacon. It may look like food poisoning to some, but it is a joy for me to behold. He climbs back under the sheets with me and gives me an I'm sorry glance as he presents me with the best of what was left of his cooking venture.

"It's the thought that counts," I tell him with a smile. He takes my face in his hands and kisses me with an intensity I will never be prepared for, but I love it deeply.

As he leans away, he has a dreamy, far-off daze in his eyes, "I just can't believe this is actually happening." We push the tray of food to the side and dedicate a good solid five minutes to making out like we're teenagers again. When we break for air he looks into my face, this time with a bittersweet smile,

"Vannah, why did you leave?"

A red flush climbs into my cheeks. It's an answer I owe him, but not one I want to give. I slump down and cover my head with the sheet so he can't see my face, "A lot of reasons. I was broken after everything with mom and I just needed to get away from this place that reminded me of her everywhere I went."

"But you could have told me. I would have followed you anywhere. You knew that, or at least I thought you did."

I bite the bullet and just say it, "I... I thought you cheated."

He can't hide his shock and he seems to be at a loss for words. He collects himself, but still doesn't quite know what to say, "Just... why?"

"There were all these people talking. All around town they were all whispering about it. I don't know where it came from or why, but it was there and it really got in my head..." I trail off because I'm beginning to put some mental pieces together again. "I saw you at dinner with Gabby. I don't know why I just assumed the worst. I should have given you a chance. I honestly don't know what happened. I..." I search my mind for answers, "I remember I got a note in my mailbox telling me to go to the restaurant." This realization strikes me as odd. I had completely forgotten the note had ever existed until now. I delve down deeper and dig for more, "There were other notes too, all in our mailbox. I would get home before Shane and I would always check the mail. I think I got a new note almost every day for a while. They all said awful things about you, us. I was already feeling insecure because of all the talk and... They said you weren't who I thought you were. They said you had a secret and you were kind of acting weird so I got all wrapped up in it. It all kind of fell together and then I saw you two together and it stuck." As I say it, all of it comes flooding back like a dam has broken. I remember all the notes turning me against the man I loved one by one. Then the next batch of memories comes into focus, years of Colby telling me how lucky I was to have stumbled on the scene and then that first time that I can clearly see I was manipulated into thinking the notes were all in my head. The broken record of him telling me the idea of the notes was probably just my suspicions taking on a life of their own in my mind. Telling me it was probably my overactive imagination. That was the start of making me feel fragile and crazy in the very beginning of our relationship. That was how he got in. It was a complete and total mind fuck.

Cash has sat silently letting me process all my thoughts, "It was him, wasn't it?" I nod. He looks disgusted. "I knew it. I knew it would all come back to him." He hugs me close to him and kisses my hair. Looking at me again, "He was obsessed with you, you know. He used to watch you. I always tried to be good to him because I knew how everyone else talked about him behind his back, but it got to be too much. We had it out because it was getting weird. That was about a month before you left." He looks a little nervous before he continues, "I wondered if maybe you were with him because he left right after you did and then you showed back up here with him and... I was so jealous."

"Cash, no. He only showed up in St. Louis about 5 years ago. I don't know where he was until then."

I can see the wheels turning in Cash's head, "Where is he now?"

"He left to stay with his mom for a while, trying to reconnect with her I think."

Cash's eyes flash, "No, he isn't. His mom died a couple of years ago. It was an overdose. I found her on a welfare check." All the pieces come together in front of us, "I fucking knew it was all him." It all sinks in for us both and we share a look of complete understanding until a loud banging on the front door startles us both, "I'll go see who it is, you stay here until I know it's safe." He grabs his gun and leaves the room.

A few moments pass and then I hear an unfamiliar voice. I peek around the bedroom door and have a clear shot of the front door. Cash is talking to another police officer, this one in uniform. The conversation seems calm enough, but Cash is tense. Wanting to know what's happening, I pull Cash's t-shirt over my head and stumble into my leggings before rushing to his side. The other officer is apologizing and reaching for his cuffs.

He looks at the officer with pleading eyes, "Joel, can I have just two seconds?" The young cop glances at me hesitantly, but nods. Cash's eyes are wide and afraid, "They found another body and there is some kind of evidence that is substantial enough to warrant my arrest for it."

Officer Joel has decided that time is up and begins speaking calmly and clearly as he places Cash in handcuffs, "You have the right to remain silent. Anything you say, can and will be used against you. You have a right..."

Cash talks over him, begging me to hear him, "You know this isn't me, Vannah. You know this is a mistake. Call Shane. Tell him what's happened. He'll know what to do." I think he might be about to cry as he says once more, "You know this isn't me."

And I do know. I know more clearly than ever that it isn't him. I have complete clarity for the first time in years.

I call Shane the second I watch Cash being put into the back of a police cruiser.

The moment Shane answers, I give him everything I know without hesitation, "It was Colby. I have no doubt. He's after

Cash. Somehow he's made it look like Cash did it all. They just took Cash away in handcuffs and he said you would know what to do."

"Fuck. Okay. Let me wrap my head around this and I'll get him out. I want you back here, now."

"No. No way. I'm going to the police station. I'm going to tell them everything I can to help."

He blows out a deep sigh, "Fine, but be careful."

"I know. I will."

We hang up as I am struggling to put on a bra and get myself in an at least semi-composed for public state. I go into the bathroom and splash water onto my face before taking a long hard look in the mirror. I stare into my own face, so happy just this morning, now distraught and unsure how to undo all that my own willful ignorance has brought about.

I was manipulated brilliantly, but did I have to let myself be molded so easily into the perfect victim? I used to be strong and independent. How did I become such pliable putty in his hands? This is not how this ends. I won't let him win.

Just as I make this pact with myself, I see a flash of movement behind me in the mirror. Please tell me Cash has a cat... I hear noise rise from the kitchen now and my blood runs cold. Where is my cell phone? I left it on the bed and the kitchen stands between it and me because why would it end up any other way? I will never again make fun of the fumbling girl in a horror movie again.

I search my surroundings for anything I can use as a weapon and think for a brief second that the plunger might be all I have at my disposal. Then my eyes land on the gleaming white toilet. I grab the lid off the tank and hold it over my head like a baseball bat. Its heavy weight wears on my arms almost immediately, but I push through the burning muscles as I make my way down the hallway.

Suddenly, the noise has now relocated to just behind me. I turn to face it, but a sudden burst of pain hits me instead. My ears ring and my brain buzzes. I feel my makeshift weapon clatter to the floor as my whole world goes black.

# III

# INTO THE DARK

*"Madness is like gravity. All it takes is a little push."*
*–The Joker*

# 27

## Savannah

My consciousness fades in and out and I can hear a constant drip of water somewhere nearby. It's dark and cold, but I am not alone. I keep seeing her. She stands just outside of the light around me and watches. She is just close enough to see the silhouette of her long curly hair and childish body. I can't make out her face because I only see her in flashes when the darkness clears my eyes. This is the longest I have been alert and I think I may be coming out of wherever I've been. I look around and see dark concrete walls surrounding me. Everything shines with dull dampness. My head is killing me. I reach up to touch the place of exploding pain but my hands won't move. Surveying my body, I see that I'm tied to the chair I'm sitting in.

Shit. My skin is streaked with blood and I am tied to a chair.

"Help me," I begin screaming out before I even know what I'm doing. I didn't even know my voice could be that loud until I hear it echoing back at me in this tomb.

"No one can hear you," a sweet voice calls out from the darkness. I jerk my head to the side and see the little girl standing just behind my shoulder. She is so close now that I could touch her if my hands were free, "Mommy told me not to scream because no one could hear me and it would only make my throat hurt." She's so very tiny and her skin is so pale that she nearly glows, even in this dark place. She reaches out and touches my hair, "You look like mommy."

"You look like me," I respond breathlessly, then seize my opportunity, "Can you please untie me, sweetie?"

The girl looks around nervously and then reaches down to help me. Just as her dirty, delicate fingers touch the tethers around my wrists, there is a loud banging in the distance. She immediately jumps back with wide, terrified eyes. Before I know what's happening she disappears into the darkness around us again.

My breathing quickens as her fear seeps into me as well. I start to struggle against the ropes and the chair begins to rock noisily against the concrete floor.

"Shhhhh... it's the bad man," her voice whispers from the darkness.

I go completely still as his heavy footsteps grow louder, thud... thud... thud... until he is just past the line of darkness. Slowly his figure comes into shape before his face finally drifts into the light. For a moment, I feel relief to see Colby's face but then it all rushes back with the force of a hurricane. He smiles and my mouth goes dry.

"You have no idea how long I have wanted to see you tied up like this," he says appreciatively. He walks over to me slowly like he may untie me after all, but he only checks to see if the ropes are all still tight, "I won't keep you like this forever, just until you know it won't do any good to run. You'll get there eventually. They always do."

It all sinks in and feels like being buried alive. He leans in to kiss my nose and I want to throw up in his face. I want to tear him apart. I plead, "Why?! I don't understand!"

"You never did understand. We could have avoided all of this. I tried to do it all the right way. I tried so fucking hard, Savannah. I said what I knew you wanted to hear. I pretended to be the nice guy. Why couldn't you just love me?"

The blood in my veins throbs inside me like icy knives, "I did love you. I thought you were the nice guy. You didn't have to do this."

He laughs and shakes his head, "Oh, but I did. I really thought we were getting there then you got that call to come home and I knew it had all been a lie. The idea of coming home turned on a light inside you that I hadn't seen since before you left. It was always him," he shakes his head in disgust, "so I had to take things into my own hands."

"The little girl, why? Let her go. Please. Keep me, but let her go back to her family." I know first hand what it feels like for a loved one to vanish. I can't bear the thought of what that little girl's family is going through. His laugh at her mention says he doesn't give a shit.

"I am her family," he says with a smirk, "She was born here. Come here, Lucy." The little girl comes to his side.

"Hi," she says feebly with a small wave toward me.

"Lucy, this lady is going to be your new mommy," Colby tells her in a singsong voice.

"But I love my first mommy," she squeaks out.

Colby slaps her face so hard that she falls to the ground and I let out a shriek of horror. He remains completely cool and collected, "She broke the rules so I had to kill her, remember? That is why you always obey the rules."

Lucy climbs off the ground with tears in her eyes. What life has this poor girl lived? My mind flashes to the girl in the woods. Was Seraphina her mom? Is Colby her father? How many have there been? What horrible things has he done in here?

"Trying to piece it all together?" he asks with a devilish grin. "It all started in 2006."

He watches me for a long moment as the gravity of that statement hits me with a bone-cracking intensity right in the middle of my chest. I know exactly what he's telling me and I don't want to give him the satisfaction of a reaction, but I'm finding it hard to breathe. I scream at him, "What did you do to her?!"

Colby laughs, "A lot."

I feel sick to my stomach, "I don't understand why," I manage to croak out.

Colby comes slowly closer to me and seems to really consider this answer, "It was always you for me. I just wanted you, but the opportunity to steal her appeared instead." He shrugs his shoulders, "She looked enough like you that it wasn't hard to pretend she was you. I thought she was at first, when I saw her walking behind the trailer to sneak a smoke. I got so excited that I just had to have her right then and didn't see it was your mom until after," he stares off into the distance almost wistfully, "She used to fight me pretty hard in the beginning, but she got used to it after the first couple of years."

"Years?!" I feel like that realization might kill me.

His laugh is a near cackle now, "Oh, sweetheart. She was alive until yesterday. That hand was hers."

Shock, disgust, and anguish flood my body in cataclysmic ways. All those years she was here. He had her locked down here like an animal. Suddenly I wish I had looked harder. I wish

I had stayed here and scoured every inch of dirt until I found her. I could have saved her. All those years.

The sounds coming out of me now are that of pure heartbreak. I haven't screamed out like this since I was a child.

Colby comes to comfort me. I want to pull away but his knots hold me in place as he strokes my face. His touch repulses me and I bite his hand.

He slaps my face just as he did Lucy's, but he smiles, "Still feisty. I love it. I'm going to let you process all this for a while. I'll come back later, love," he says as he leans down to whisper in my ear, "Maybe then I'll get us reacquainted."

His hand slides up my thigh as he says it and I feel bile rise in my throat. He laughs again and then disappears behind me. I can hear him shuffling around behind me and wish more than anything I could walk up behind him to tear him to shreds. I want to eviscerate him. I want to erase his presence off this earth.

His hand on my shoulder again makes me jump and hold my breath. Whispering in my ear he says, "I want you to sleep while I'm gone so you don't wear yourself out screaming. No one can hear you anyway."

He licks my ear and I stiffen as I feel the burning stick of a needle in my neck. Within seconds I feel the world slipping away from me again. My mind claws and screams to stay in the here and now, but the cold numbness of anesthesia crawls over me until there's nothing left but empty space and my mother's face.

This must be what it feels like to drown.

# 28

# Savannah

This is such a strange sense of consciousness. Everything is black, but I can still hear things around me, I think some of it might be real. I know some of it isn't, but I'm not conscious enough to know the difference.

Something feels cool against my lips and the cold seems to be spreading down my throat. I can feel it settling in my stomach like liquid nitrogen in my core, making me shiver all over. The icy jolt is enough to pry my tired eyelids open and I can see Colby in front of me, forcing water through my lips. His close proximity causes me to gasp in surprise and the icy cold water floods my lungs as well. Coughing and spluttering, I spray Colby with the water. In an instant, the rest of it in the cup is thrown in my face. It hurts everywhere like needles stabbing into me and is enough to drag me firmly back into the here and now. Gasping for breath, I blink through the water and shriek out in disgust for the man in front of me.

Colby is livid, "Be a little grateful for what I'm trying to give you!" He is out of his mind with rage.

I scream out, "You are a piece of shit!" My words echo

between us and something in him visibly snaps.

He lets out a guttural growl as he charges at me, his hands wrapping around my throat. The impact of his rush on my body knocks my chair backward and we both fall to the floor. Still tied, arms and legs to this chair, he straddles me and completely cuts off my air supply. The pressure in my chest and head as he tries to squeeze the life out of me is immense. I feel as though my lungs might collapse in on themselves while my eyes find a way to pop out of my head.

This is it. I am sure this is how I die, at the hands of the mad man that took my mother away as well. My insides are screaming and bright starbursts begin to take over my vision, but then... it just stops.

I gasp for air as Colby, now cool and collected, releases my throat and stands up, leaving me in my overturned chair panting and gasping as I stare at the dirt ceiling.

After a few moments, he comes back over and sets my chair upright. He then kneels to face me, eye to eye, "You make it extremely hard for me to keep my cool, my dear, but I have worked too hard for too long to just give you up like that." He reaches out and runs his fingers over the cold, dirty skin of my cheek, "No, I have big plans for us."

"I don't understand why you are doing this," I sputter through my now rough and scratchy throat.

"Because you are supposed to be mine and you won't just fucking go with it," he explodes as his voice begins to ramp up with anger once more, but he makes an effort to shrug it off, "I had children with her, you know." My stomach turns at his words and he smiles, "Sera and Lucy? They are your sisters, Savannah. There have been others too, but they didn't make it." He explains it all like it's no big deal, "I've had a whole life down here for 14 years and not a single soul had a clue. Mind-blowing, isn't it?" He looks wistful now, "Growing my seed in a woman's womb. That is, without a doubt, the greatest feeling in the world. I'm so ready to share that with you. I know you've been secretly taking birth control at home, but down here... down here I get to control your body. Our babies will be so beautiful, Savannah."

There is nothing I can do to fully process his insane thoughts. I can't even hear his plans for me. All I can think about is Mom, "Why did you kill her? You've had her down here all this time, why kill her now?"

"The girl in the woods? Seraphina? She was the first baby your mom had down here. I was amazed when she survived after what I put Beth through while she was pregnant. I had no use for a baby back then so I made her go away, but the need for her arose again recently. All thanks to you, babe," he laughs, as if all of this is just a fun game to him, "I brought her down here with me that first night we were back in town. Your mom got to watch all the fun things I did to her. I guess she got antsy seeing it happen to someone else. Wasn't too long before I caught your mom telling little Lucy to try and get out. I guess maybe she noticed I was a little more distracted than usual, thanks for that by the way, and I lost my temper a little. I lopped her hand off before I had any time to really think it through and she bled out overnight," he shrugs it off nonchalantly, "I was sad to see her go. We had shared so many years, but I had already decided to bring you down here by then so it was okay. It really worked out having the hand too. I was able to make Cash look even more guilty. It was all very artistic, don't you think? The ring he bought for you on your mom's hand? Brilliant." He smirks now, "I may officially have you, but I still want him to rot."

What he has done to my family is unforgivable. Atrocious. Disgusting. My heart is shattered in my chest weeping along-side me. I drop my head because I just can't look at him anymore. That movement jolts my chair and that's when I feel it. The tiniest little wiggle of instability. Within a split second my eyes have opened wider and I have formulated a plan in my now crystal clear mind. Lucy and I will not die at his hands. We are broken beyond repair, but we won't let him win. If there is a chance for us to turn this around together, we will make it happen.

With my eyes still focusing on my own lap, I spit my words at him like venom, "I have never really loved you." It comes out almost a whisper as I gather any strength I have buried somewhere inside me, "I could never love you." My voice rises in volume with every word and I raise my head to look him directly in his soulless eyes, "You are a miserable excuse for a man and I want nothing more than to see you rot in hell." I can see his resolve twitching, but I'm not quite hitting the right nerve to get the reaction I want just yet. With a smile fueled by madness creeping across my lips, I nail him where it seems to hurt him most, "Every time you fucked me, I saw his face. It was never you. I always pretended it was Cash." The anger boiling up inside him is visible now and I continue, waiting for that inevitable explosion, "He's the only reason I came back here. He and I had a plan. I would come back here to be with him and make you look like a fool. You will never, ever, make me feel good like Cash can."

There it is.

White-hot fury bursts out of him in a scream of anger as he rushes at me again. This time he plants a kick directly to my chest. It completely knocks the air from my lungs and I hear the

153

bones creak and crack, but I get what I want and smile through the pain as my chair tumbles backward once more. It slams against the floor and rattles every bone in my body, but it will be worth it.

"Why? Why does he continue to be this annoying little gnat buzzing through my life?!" Colby has lost all control. He yells and screams at me while pacing like a caged animal, "He doesn't deserve you! He doesn't deserve anything!" With that, he storms out and leaves me lying on the cold ground.

Excellent.

# 29

# Savannah

I sit silently and perfectly still, waiting. I strain my ears to hear his footsteps as they stomp into the distance. When their sound fades away to nothing, I slowly count to 100 in my head. No sign of his return has materialized so I begin to wiggle and squirm in my now broken chair. The hard impacts on the concrete floor have weakened all the joints and cracked some of the wooden legs. Pretty quickly, as I stretch and twist my body against the broken thing, it falls to pieces. My arms are free to cross my body and start untying the ropes holding me here.

"I can help you?" questions the tiny voice from the shadows.

"Sweet, beautiful girl. Yes, please help me. I'm going to take you away from all of this down here."

Lucy smiles so brightly and in an instant I know I would do anything in the world for her.

"Are we going up there?" she asks, pointing above us, " I've never been up there before."

My hands are free now and I reach out to embrace her so tight. She never asked for this life, "I'll take you up there, sweetheart.

Can you show me how the bad man gets in and out of here?"

Lucy nods her head enthusiastically, so happy to be helpful, and motions for me to follow her. I survey the broken chair first and pick out a piece of the sharp, jagged broken leg with nails jutting out of it at odd angles. This will work perfectly. Holding my impromptu weapon over my head like a baseball bat, I follow Lucy into pitch-black darkness.

The dim room we had been in shrinks down to a tunnel. What is this place? Lucy seems to know every turn even blind in the darkness. Watching her, barely visible even just inches from me, methodically cruise through this abyss like it's nothing is mesmerizing. I guess, though, if I had lived my entire life here I would know my way around too. This is her home.

Finally, we come to a stop and Lucy points straight up toward the ceiling 3 feet above us. Right there, emitting a faint glow of warm light is some sort of round plate.

There is no way I can reach that. Fuck.

My mind races trying to find a way to reach this hole and out of this hell. I look at Lucy's expectant face and ask, "Is there any furniture in here? Chairs? A table? A bed?"

Lucy shakes her head and stares up at me looking for answers that I just don't have. Wracking my brain, I try to think of any possibility.

I could lift Lucy on my shoulders and hope she is strong enough to move the metal cover, but what if Colby is still out there and sees her tiny face climbing out of the hole? What would he do once she got up there? Are we even remotely near anyone that could help? The idea that Colby might still be up there hits me again. My stomach clinches in knots and I have no idea what to do.

"Is there any other place that looks like this?" I ask, pointing to the glowing circle above us. Lucy shakes her head. With a deep steadying sigh, I make a decision.

I raise the piece of broken chair toward the metal plate above us and am overjoyed to see it reaches, even if just barely. On my very tiptoes, I can push it enough to raise it just a fraction. Every time I budge it sunshine pours in from above. If only I was a couple of inches taller... with a last look at Lucy's sweet face I summon all my strength and jump toward the ceiling with the broken chair upraised. The metal cover pops up before coming down to land slightly off-center of where it began. A thick sliver of sunshine pours in on us, warming our faces. Lucy giggles and moves her hands through the warm light. It is the most delightful sound I can imagine and I smile back at her.

What will happen if Colby is still here and sees the lid popping off? I'll bash his head in, that's what.

Jump after jump, I move the lid a little more each time until finally it is almost entirely out of sight. Sunshine streams down on us. Lucy's eyes are full of wonder and joy as she stares up at the blue sky and fluffy white clouds. I will never look at the world the same after seeing it through her eyes. I'm getting her out of here and showing her everything.

If Colby's erratic personality hasn't reacted by now, he must not still be up there. I kneel in front of Lucy and look her in the eyes, "I'm going to put you on my shoulders and lift you up. Can you climb out of the hole if I do that?"

Lucy nods her head yes, so excited.

"When you get up there, can you try to find something for me to climb up on?"

Nodding again, she climbs on my shoulders with ease. I stand and find her much lower compared to the opening than I had anticipated. She reaches for the ground above us and can just barely grasp it with her fingertips.

"Okay, listen. I'm going to help you stand on my shoulders. It might feel scary but you've got this. Okay?"

"Okay," Lucy squeaks out as she nods again, her eyes sparkling.

I place her feet in my hands and realize for the first time that she is barefoot, feet dirty and rough with thick callouses. Such a small detail, especially at this moment, but it guts me. Has she ever owned a pair of shoes in her life? I shake off my despair and use it to fuel the extra strength I need to lift her small frame over my head. She squirms for a moment as her shaky legs try to hold her up, but then her weight lifts itself off my palms and I watch her wiggle her way out of this hell hole that she has called home.

Her giggles are exhilarating, "I did it! I really did it!"

I can't help but let a smile stretch across my face, "Yes, you did! You are amazing!" She goes quiet now and her shadow disappears from my sight, "Lucy, can you hear me, sweetie?"

A few moments of silence go by and I begin to fret and worry. What if he was still up there? What if he got her and is about to throw her lifeless body back down to me? My stomach begins to twist and knot itself, but then I hear her, "I found it! I found it!"

With her words come a black cargo ladder down into the hole. I scream out in joy and clamor my way up. As I reach hand over hand toward the sunshine, my adrenaline rush wavers and the weight of pain in my body nearly consumes me. I begin to fear that I may not be able to lift my body out of here, but then I look up to see her hopeful little face beaming down at me. I push through what I am feeling physically and drag myself up one rung at a time.

I heave my body onto the damp, cold ground and Lucy rushes to hug me, "Thank you," she says again and again through her sobs. I hug her so tight. She holds inside her a piece of my mother that I never got to know.

She and I stand up together, hand in hand, and survey our surroundings. Good news and bad news. I know exactly where we are, but it is miles to the closest house.

I bend down to Lucy's level and look her in the eyes, "We are going to have to walk for a very long time, okay?" She nods her head. "I promise I will keep you safe, okay?" She nods again. "Can you put the ladder back where you found it?" She immediately scoops it up, unhooking it from two small notches sticking up from the ground, and runs over to stuff it into a large hole in the trunk of an old oak tree. I turn to look back toward the hole we just came out of and wonder how in the world no one knew this place existed, but as I work to hide the evidence of our exit and replace the lid, I see how perfectly camouflaged it is with the ground. When I have it placed back where it belongs you would never know anything is out of the ordinary. It's perfect, down to dried leaves and blades of grass affixed to the top. Plus, I am certain this is land owned by Colby's family. That asshole thought of everything. I close my eyes and shake off the sick taste he puts in my mouth. I reach for Lucy's hand, "Are you ready?" She chews her lip and looks up at me with uncertainty in her eyes. I bend to her level again, "What is it, sweetheart?"

"What's your name?"

Oh my goodness. She is so pure and perfect. I kneel on the ground in front of her so we are eye to eye, "My name is Savannah. My friends call me Vannah or Savvy."

She smiles softly, "Mommy talked about you. Am I your

friend?"

"Even better. I'm your sister."

Her smile brightens and she throws her arms around my neck, "I'm ready now."

With that, off we go. Thankfully, I know these woods like the back of my hand, even after all these years. All of us that grew up in this town do. We partied and got up to no good out here. I spent many nights cuddled up by a bonfire with Cash in the next field over from where Lucy and I just crawled out of the Earth, yet we never knew what was right under our feet. We searched the nearby woods when my mom was missing and she was right here, just out of sight. The thought fills me with so much regret. She was right here. Why didn't we look harder... but I just can't go there right now. I still have Lucy to save. At least I can do that. I glance down at her by my side. I can tell she is growing tired, but she never complains. Every time I check on her she smiles up at me, beaming. It's every bit of motivation I need.

We reach the top of another hill and through the trees, I see the old grey farmhouse that I have been picturing in my mind for what must be at least an hour. It's enough to make me cry. It looks exactly like I remember it, hopefully, that means Mrs. Brinkman still lives there. She must be in her sixties by now, but she was genuinely good and kind. I know she would be an ally. Here's also hoping she remembers who I am...

I am so excited that I scoop Lucy up into my arms and run the last hundred yards or so to the front door. There on her little front porch, I see the mailbox, D. Brinkman. I have never been so grateful in all my life. I frantically start knocking on the door until I see her peeking out the window. She opens the door with lines of worry across her forehead. I can only imagine what we must look like to this little old woman.

160

"Mrs. Brinkman, hi... I don't know if you remember me but...
"

She gives me a confused smile, "I know who you are, Savannah. What's wrong? What's happened to you and your little friend?"

I release a tremendous sigh, "Too much to ever explain," tears choke me as I try to talk and the kind woman reaches out for my hand. "Can you please look after my friend, Lucy, and call 911?"

"Of course, love. Come inside, nothing to worry about."

"I- I can't come in," sobs now punctuate every word I say and I have no control over them. "I have to go help someone else, but I have to go alone. Please can you help?"

Her hand covers her mouth and she nods solemnly. Lucy looks up at me frightened.

I sit on my knees in front of her, "Mrs. Brinkman is our friend. She's a very nice woman. I trust her and you can too. Can you stay with her while I go help another friend?"

She doesn't respond, just moves her eyes back and forth from me to the old woman. Her whole existence she has only ever known two people, Mommy and the bad man. I can't begin to imagine how overwhelming this is for her.

Mrs. Brinkman extends her hand to Lucy, "I have known your friend, Savannah, since she was about your size, dear. I was her teacher. I'll take care of you sweetheart."

Lucy looks reluctantly at the outstretched hand and then back to me. I give her a reassuring smile and she places her hand in the woman's.

"Thank you," I plead as I stand and make my way back down the stairs, "Please call 911. Right now. Tell them to send officers here and officers to Cash's house."

Her face is full of grave concern, but she nods and ushers Lucy into the house. I know that she will be safe here because I am certain I know exactly where Colby is.

# 30

# Savannah

I pretty much set Cash up for Colby to pay him a visit. I pushed and prodded at all of Colby's buttons to get him out of there and didn't entirely consider the consequences. I used the only words I could think of to make him as mad as I needed him in that moment. I can only hope now, as I begin making my way through the trees again, that Cash is still safely tucked away in a jail cell. Knowing my own brother though, I fear he has already been returned home on bail. If so, I pray he saw Colby coming in time and that he can ever forgive me for throwing him under the bus.

The run from Mrs. Brinkman's house to Cash's is short as I cut through patches of trees, across old dirt roads, and then through random backyards as I make my way back into town. I am astonished but thrilled to know that I still remember every last inch of this place I thought I had forgotten. It seems the years of scattering from underage field parties have paid off tremendously.

Seeing Cash's house come into view, I feel another adrenaline jolt buzz through my body and my feet begin to run faster.

The implications of what I did, what I had to do, to save myself and Lucy pound over and over in my head matching my heavy footfalls. It had to be done, but at what cost? What if Shane bailed Cash out, brought him home, and they both got ambushed? What if they are both laying dead by Colby's hands because of me?

My feet speed up again, trying to fly me to where I need to be.

Finally here, I peer around the neighbor's giant hedges, now the only thing between myself and the house. I have no idea what to expect, but I don't see Shane's car anywhere nearby and everything looks normal. Still, something feels off. There is a sort of primal weight to the air. It seems thick with hateful tension. Cutting my way through it, I tiptoe to the backdoor and silently slip inside.

I take in everything around me, trying to develop plans as I go. Papers from the counter are scattered on the kitchen floor. The trash can has been knocked over, letting trash spill across the cold tile. I approach the hallway and see shards of glass and a shattered picture frame. There are smears of blood down the wall and I feel a tight squeeze in my stomach, but the silence gives me no way of knowing if this is all new or from my own struggle... it feels like a hundred years have passed since then... but then I hear it.

From the living room, harsh whispers cut the silence like a sharp knife. A guttural growl then crashes through the air and I rush to join the scene as silently as possible. The voices grow louder as I slink through the shadows and I can now clearly identify with certainty the two men in the midst of this showdown. Just before the pair comes into sight, I pass Cash's work gear hanging on the hallway coat rack. A quick scan reveals no gun, but then the baseball bat leaning against the wall behind the coat rack shines out to me like a beacon. I reach for it greedily and try to maneuver it out without making any sound.

Bat in hand, I peer around the corner into the living room. The scene is like a hot blade through my core. Furniture is on its side, the TV is smashed, and there is blood everywhere. Most of the precious red liquid seems to have spilled out of the massive crack in Cash's head. His color is pale and waxy. His eyes are heavy and bloodshot as they rise to meet mine for just a brief second. I do everything I can to convey a plan to him in that instant. He must receive some kind of message as he seems to rally any strength he has left.

Licking his dried lips, he begins trying to talk Colby down, "You don't have to do this, man."

The rough, wounded scratch in his voice fills me with even more loathing for the monster that did this to him and for myself for bringing him back into Cash's life.

Colby growls out a response and I see red, "Watching you slowly bleed out until every ounce of life has drained out of you will be the greatest pleasure of my life."

He leans toward Cash, watching his head wound pulse out more and more blood, and I capitalize on the moment. Throwing myself into the room I smash the bat against Colby's head with the full strength of my whole soul. The hard thwack is accompanied by a brittle crunch and he falls to the floor with a groan. He stares up at me with stunned fear and I know that's how I want him to die. I want his last breath to be taken in fear, just like he made my mother and sister endure.

Lost in anger, grief, and so much pain, I cry out like a wild woman and bring the bat down on him again and again. I've lost all control and continue to beat him until an unnatural dent appears in his skull.

I am hysterical, sweating, and still full of rage, but Cash's rough voice brings me back to reality pretty quickly, "Vannah, it's okay. You can stop."

I let the bat fall from my hands and clatter to the floor. Turning to face the man I love, have always loved, I see the true gravity of his condition once again. I rush to his side and wrap my arms around his waist to help support his weight. He tries to smile, but he doesn't have much left to give.

"Cash, I am so sorry," I wail as tears pour down my face.

"This wasn't on you, Vannah," he manages to express and as the last bit of color drains from his face, "I loved you my whole life." His words sound like a goodbye as I collapse to the ground under the weight of his now limp body.

Holding him in my arms, I try everything I can think of to rouse him from this bloody slumber, but there seems to be nothing left inside him. An empty vessel.

I'm still screaming his name when the police finally arrive and drag me away from his body.

# 31

# Epilogue

This story doesn't have a happy ending.

What in life ever does? There is no way, in reality, to tie up all the loose ends. You can't pack it all up in a box and hide it with a pretty bow. Sometimes bad things happen and it just is what it is. What can you do?

As I sit in this sterile room listening to the buzzes and beeps of the machines keeping him alive, I can't help but feel the sting of life's utter unfairness. I spent so many years hating him for things he never even did. I lost all that time with him and now it's too late. I'll never get the chance to make up for leaving. I put the burden of assumed guilt on his shoulders for too many years and I will never have the opportunity to apologize for that. Just one of many regrets I have in the aftermath of Hurricane Colby. I can't believe he got away with so much for so many years. He dictated all the details of our lives and we had no idea.

I sit here every day, looking at the empty shell of a man who loved me so much that he let me hate him just to make me feel better, and I can't even cry. I have no tears left. I'm numb. I have to choose that for myself or I risk coming a little too unraveled to function. I'm sure my therapist would have lots to say about that choice of coping mechanism.

Sweet Lucy has been doing so much better than myself though. I am so proud of the strong soul that she is. She's filled with giggles and smiles that light up my world. For Lucy, everything is a novelty and seeing it with her brightens even the darkest of moments. Of course she has her own personal demons thanks to the life she lived, but she is seeing a counselor in addition to all the Department of Family Services advocates they've sent our way since that day I brought her into the sunshine. Considering, she is adjusting quite well.

Lucy, Shane, and I talk about our mom a lot. Shane and I share stories of our time with her and Lucy does the same. The stories are vastly different in devastating ways but are cathartic and still share a common thread. Our mother was wonderful. Even in the hell pit they were kept in and after so much brutal abuse, she still showed love in a profound way. I think that is a big reason why Lucy is doing so well. She was raised by a woman that made her feel secure and loved even in the worst of all circumstances. That detail gives me so much joy. He was never able to break my mother. No matter what he did physically, Beth Raymore never let him take away her soul.

He posed her body in the middle of the city park surrounded by various paraphernalia to incriminate Cash in her murder. His t-shirt on her body. His cellphone carelessly dropped on the scene. Personal photos of Cash and I together. A letter that sounded like nothing but the rantings of a man descending into madness, but signed with the nearly illegible name, Cash. At first glance, the scene screamed Cash's guilt, but that all quickly dissolved when Colby's fingerprints and even DNA turned up on all of it. He even left his own prints on her body.

Her autopsy revealed that she had been crippled years ago, likely intentionally, and was completely unable to walk. She also showed evidence of years and years of severe abuse and malnutrition. Between what I know of Colby's life over the last handful of years and what the police have found, we have been able to piece together that he likely only brought food once a month when he would tell me he was traveling for work. He would spend several days down there with his victims, making up for lost time since he had last been there. They had to fend for themselves the rest of the time and make whatever he brought last. They never knew when or if he would ever be back.

The fact that no one ever found this little homemade lair is nothing but sheer luck on Colby's part. He did little to nothing to protect his secret, other than living a double life. He had average intelligence but was over confident. There were no safeguards in place to protect him. He was simply lucky. It makes you wonder how many other despicable things go on under our noses every single day. It's sickening.

I try not to continuously get caught in the loop of how unfair it all is, but looking at the dying man laying in front of me just keeps bringing it all back to the surface with a stinging burn, like ripping off a bandaid over and over. There are just so many things I wish I could change.

My Cash. My love.

I wish I had more to offer him than just my shattered self, but I know he understands. As I look into his face, I know he will always will. I am so thankful to have his shoulder to cry on when I leave my father's bedside every night. He walks into the room just now and hands me my perfect cup of coffee making my heart skip a beat. The idea that our love could still beat this strong after so long and so much is beyond miraculous.

He kisses my head as he walks by and goes to place a hand over my dad's. The two men developed a close friendship while I was gone and Cash is grieving this impending loss as hard as a son would.

I rise from my chair, aching from far too little sleep, and cross the room to stand by his side. He drapes his arm over my shoulder and I nuzzle into that perfect little nook that I swear was made just for me. With a kiss to my head, he tells me, "Lucy is with Shane and Gabby."

I smile, "Thank you. How is she today?"

"Good. Hungry. Would you ladies like to have dinner with me?"

"I hate to leave him..."

"Shane said he'll come trade places with you."

He knows me so well, has my answer before I even ask the question, "That sounds wonderful then."

I lean down and kiss my dad on the cheek then take Cash's hand. As we are walking out the door, Shane is coming in the room. We exchange sad smiles as we pass. Lucy looks up from the book Gabby is reading to her and we lock eyes. She grins ear to ear and runs to greet me. I scoop her up in my arms and relish her tight squeeze around my neck. She lets me go to reach for Cash and squeals when he snatches her into his arms. I think she may love him as much as I do and that makes my heart feel full. Gabby squeezes my arm as she walks by to join Shane in Dad's room. Cash and I walk hand in hand down the cold corridor but our little trio is nothing but warm.

The trauma inflicted on all the people I love never should have happened. We will never be exactly who we were before it all. I will never get the lost ten years of my life back. Lucy can never erase her horrific beginnings. Cash will forever live with a physical scar from the day we almost lost him. The grief felt by Shane and I over the tragedy that was our parent's lives will never heal. None of those things are okay or forgivable. None of that allows for a truly happy ending. There's too much baggage and the hurt is too much, but we did survive and were able to salvage nearly everything being ripped away from us. We have all clung to each other and the bond our family now shares is even deeper than ever before.

The monster did not win, but love did and that is as close to happy as we can get. Shane and I will mourn our mother and the atrocities committed against her for the rest of our lives, but we will also love her Lucy for the rest of our lives. We will wish we had known our sister, Seraphina, every moment of every day, but we will never let her memory die.

I will never stop wishing I had a second chance with my dad, but I will always know how well Shane and Cash took care of him in my absence. There will never be a day that I don't regret how I treated Shane and Gabby, but they will never stop being my family. A part of me will always hate myself for the things I said and did to the man I love, but through all of the sadness and all of the grief, he will be there. We will all walk through the rest of our days together. I ran from that for far too long.

Now, as Cash and I sit in this crowded hospital cafeteria, he looks at me with the same fire in his eyes that he held for me when we were 15 and I know everything will be okay.

It will never be perfect, but it will be okay.

# About the Author

Amanda East is a lifetime lover of words. She has filled her world with them, devouring books and crafting tales since before she can remember. Now, she continues to share that love with her children and husband in the same Missouri Ozarks that she sets her stories in.

**You can connect with me on:**

☑ https://facebook.com/authorAmandaEast

# Also by Amanda East

**Delightful Fear: Tales of the Macabre**

What are you afraid of? We all have our own triggers of that crawling, sprawling tingle that is fear. In this collection of the dark and macabre, explore horrors you never imagined and maybe find your own new nightmare fuel. Are you ready to experience this Delightful Fear?

Printed in Great Britain
by Amazon